THE GIRL WHO
LIVED ALONE

By the same author

Two Men, The Book Guild, 2000
A Family Affair, The Book Guild, 2001
Forbidden, The Book Guild, 2001
The Feud, The Book Guild, 2002
The Peacock, The Book Guild 2002
Duet, The Book Guild, 2003
Two Girls, The Book Guild, 2003
Two Into One, The Book Guild, 2003
My Friend Jenni, The Book Guild, 2005
A Girl Called Peta, The Book Guild, 2007

THE GIRL WHO LIVED ALONE

And Other Stories

Peter Rogers

Book Guild Publishing
Sussex, England

First published in Great Britain in 2008 by
The Book Guild Ltd
Pavilion View
19 New Road
Brighton, BN1 1UF

Typesetting in Baskerville by
Keyboard Services, Luton, Bedfordshire

Printed in Great Britain by
CPI Antony Rowe

A catalogue record for this book is available from
The British Library

ISBN 978 1 84624 199 4

CONTENTS

THE GIRL WHO LIVED ALONE

It was not known in the market town of Bensham just how many girls lived alone either in bedsit accommodation or in an apartment without benefit of parents or any other relative. These girls were independent and self-reliant but it was not easy to imagine what kind of life they lived. A lonely one in all probability. One girl in particular, Barbara Hammond, can remember being in care as a child and asking who she could send a Christmas card to. She saw the couple sitting at the table writing cards but she had no relatives so she ended up sending a card to the two people who cared for her. She remembered it as a sad moment in her life.

But that was long ago for she now lived alone in an inexpensive block of apartments in Bensham and worked in one of the local banks as a secretary. She was a very attractive girl in her mid-twenties with dark wavy hair and an olive complexion. She had a good figure with what the boys called nice legs. She was popular with the friends she met both at work and at the tennis club and, in particular, at the Saturday dances at the local Corn Exchange. In spite of her popularity she had no regular boyfriend. The occasional visit to a cinema was as much as she could expect from any admirer. Yet she was not unduly worried. She wasn't eager to become involved in any permanent relationship. She was self-sufficient to such an extent that some people called her frigid, which was far from the truth.

It was on her return from one of the Saturday night dances at the Corn Exchange that the tragedy happened. She left the dance at midnight and drove home to her apartment, where she was in the habit of leaving the car outside in the road. It was a small second-hand car but was her pride and joy because she had just managed to complete the payments on it. It was a beautiful June night and the moon was so full that it lit up the street. She had danced almost exclusively with one young man and they had agreed to meet the next evening and go to the local cinema.

In this happy frame of mind she was just getting out of her car when a strange man came to the door and said, 'Get in.'

'I'm just going home,' said Barbara, innocently.

The man produced a knife and held it to her throat.

'Get in or you get this,' he threatened.

Barbara, cold with fear, got back into the car while the man opened the back door and got in behind her, holding the knife to the back of her neck and giving it a little prick to urge her on.

'No horn blowing and no flashing lights,' he commanded. 'Now drive.'

'Where?'

'Anywhere. Out of the town. Come on.'

Barbara started up the car and drove away slowly.

'Come on,' the man urged. 'Get a move on.'

Every now and then Barbara stole a look in the rear mirror to study the man. He was chewing gum, she noticed. He was an ordinary-looking man in a blue lounge suit. He wore no disguise and he had an educated accent.

'Do you live round here?' she asked, hoping to mollify him.

'Mind your own business.'

'I have some money in my purse if you want it.'

'Keep it.'

'I've never seen you before.'

'You may not see me again, either.'

'Where do you want to go? Do you want me to drop you somewhere?'

Brenda, in spite of the fact she was shaking with fear and her stomach was turning to water, was trying to pacify the man and eventually be free of him. By now they had left the town of Bensham and were in the country.

'That's better,' said the man.

As Barbara drove on she realised that she was completely isolated. There was just no one about. She was so frightened that if she saw someone she would stop the car and call out, risking the knife that the man still held at her neck.

Suddenly the man said, 'Pull up in that gateway.'

'Don't you want to go on?'

'Shut up. Pull up and get out.'

Barbara obediently stopped the car in the gateway that led to some farm meadow.

'Turn the lights out and get out.'

The man was already out of the car. He opened Barbara's door and flourished the wicked-looking knife again.

'Come on. Get out.'

Barbara struggled out of the car and stood facing the man.

'What now?'

'Open the gate.'

Barbara walked to the gate. By the light of the moon she could see the latch which she released and the gate swung open with a loud crack.

The man followed her into the field.

'Lie down,' he commanded.

'Oh, no. Not that,' cried Barbara.

'Get down, I tell you!'

The man pushed her so hard that she fell backwards. He was on top of her at once.

'No! No!' she shouted, trying to fight him off.

The man tore at her clothes like a maniac, not bothering to unbutton anything, even tearing her knickers away in one swipe. At the same time he was digging at her thighs and stomach with his knife. Every time she shouted or called out he punched her in the face until she was covered in blood. He seemed to have gone mad. Stunned into submission and transfixed by fear, Barbara could only cry.

When he had finished raping her he said, 'I left my bloody hood behind. I'll have to kill you.'

Barbara suddenly came to life and tried to get up but he pushed her back.

'Get back, you bitch.'

'Don't kill me. Please,' she pleaded. 'Do what you like but don't kill me.'

'I'll have to. You'll go to the police.'

'No, I won't. I promise.'

'You won't be able to help it.'

'I won't say anything to anybody.'

'You'll give them my description.'

'No, I won't. Honest.'

'Promise? Nothing.'

Suddenly he gripped her by the throat.

'Die, blast you! Die!'

Gurgling sounds issued from the girl's throat and her eyes bulged frighteningly. She kicked and struggled but the man held on to her throat, squeezing it. She threw her head back, gasping for air as his hands tightened round her throat, his thumbs digging deep into her windpipe, blocking the flow of air. Saliva bubbled in her mouth and her body suddenly went limp. The man relaxed his grip.

'About time,' the man muttered, looking down at the now lifeless body.

He got to his feet and made for the girl's car

parked in the gateway. Leaving the farm gate open, he got in and drove away. He turned the car round and drove back to Bensham where he abandoned it and made his way to his lodgings a few streets away from Barbara's home. He was pleased with himself for not only had he experienced extreme sex with the girl, he had managed to kill her, something he had never done before. He had usually used a hood as a disguise but as he'd left it behind he had no alternative but to get rid of the girl. He was surprised what a sense of exhilaration it gave him. He'd love to be able to tell his fellow cashiers at the local supermarket where he worked but he dare not.

The sun was already quite high in the sky next morning when Farmer Hardy left the house to inspect his stock of beef cattle in the Long Meadow that adjoined the main road. He did not walk but drove a kind of golf buggy across the fields. As he neared Long Meadow he saw in the distance that the gate to the road was open.

He cursed audibly: 'Eh, no! Some stupid bastard's left the gate open.'

Thinking that some of his cattle might have escaped, he increased the throttle on the buggy and bumped towards the gate. He got off the machine and shut the gate, noticing that the beasts were fortunately over the other side of the field. As he turned to get back on the buggy he saw what he thought was a bundle of bloody rags in the hedgerow. Some kid thrown it over, he assumed. He walked over to investigate. As he got closer he could see that the pile of rubbish was a girl, half naked and covered in blood.

'Christ!' he exclaimed. 'What the hell happened to you?'

The girl appeared to be dead and the farmer had visions of the police and public invading the place. But as he looked down at her he could see that she was breathing faintly, slowly. She tried to move but couldn't.

'Help,' she whispered in a hoarse, strangled voice.

'Hang on,' said the farmer. 'Let me get you home.'

'A man...' was all she could say as her throat hurt from the pressure on her windpipe.

The farmer picked her up, which made her scream with pain. He carried her to his buggy, got on and drove as fast as he could back to the farmhouse.

As soon as he arrived he called out to his wife, 'Mother! Mother!'

He got out of the buggy and carried the half-conscious girl into the house. His wife, whom he always called Mother although the children were no longer at home, was Mrs Hardy, an attractive woman of late middle age with black hair. She came hurrying into the hall.

'Charles!' she cried. 'What's happened?'

'Get an ambulance. Quick!'

While his wife hurried to the phone, Charles Hardy laid the girl gently on the sofa in the sitting room. She tried to speak but could only croak.

'Don't worry, girl. We'll get you to hospital.'

The hospital would be in Bensham and the ambulance would come from there. Tears were running down the girl's face and she sobbed uncontrollably when his wife came back into the room.

'Give her some brandy,' said Charles Hardy.

His wife went to the sideboard and poured some brandy into a glass. She took it to the girl.

'Drink this, dear.'

8

The wife put her arm round the girl's shoulders to help her reach the glass. She noticed the terrible bruising on her throat. As soon as she sipped the liquid the girl choked. She waved the glass away with a limp hand.

When the ambulance arrived the farmer explained, 'I found her like that in one of the fields. I don't know who she is or what happened.'

'Don't worry,' said the ambulance man. 'We'll take care of her.'

A stretcher was produced and the two ambulance men lifted the girl gently onto it. She cried out when she was moved because of her injuries. One of the men sat beside her as they drove to Bensham hospital.

The farmer and his wife watched the ambulance drive away.

'She's been attacked by someone,' said the farmer.

'If it's rape we should call the police,' suggested his wife.

'The hospital will do that.'

'Poor kid.'

'I thought she was dead when I saw her.'

'Good job you stopped.'

At the hospital nurses and doctors were alerted. The girl was quickly taken to the operating theatre where the knife slashes on her thighs and stomach were stitched up. The surgeon tried to look in her throat but she could not open it sufficiently. The bruises round it were black and red as if she had hanged herself. She was still unable to speak properly and could only make gurgling sounds.

The only word she could manage, and that with great difficulty, was, 'Rape.'

Once she was wheeled into one of the private wards the hospital contacted the police. The call came through to the Station Sergeant at Bensham.

'Bensham Hospital here. We have a girl here who says she's been raped.'

'Raped?' echoed the Sergeant.

'That's what I said. And she's in a pretty bad way.'

'I'll send someone over.'

'Thank you.'

The Sergeant rang through to Detective Inspector Rankin.

'Right,' said Rankin. 'I'll go over there.'

He dropped what he was doing, got in his car and drove to the hospital, where he was shown to the girl's room by one of the Sisters.

'She's almost out of her mind,' said the Sister. 'All she does is lie in bed curled up and shaking.'

'Oh, dear. Sounds bad.'

He went into the girl's room. She did not look up. Rankin stood aghast. He had never seen a girl in such a pitiful state. He turned to the Sister who had stayed with him.

'Do we know anything about her?' he asked.

'Nothing. You can see her wounds.'

Rankin sat in the chair beside the bed.

'What is your name, dear?'

The girl looked blankly at him, not seeming to understand.

'We couldn't get anything out of her,' said the Sister. 'She hasn't got a handbag or anything.'

Rankin turned to the girl.

'I'm a policeman, dear,' he said. 'I want to help you.'

The girl only curled herself up closer and said nothing.

'She can hardly speak,' warned the Sister. 'You can see she's been throttled rather badly.'

'Has the doctor examined her?'

'Not for your purposes.'

'This calls for one of our girls. I'll go back and send one over. In the meantime I don't think she should be left alone.'

'Don't worry,' promised the Sister. 'Someone will be with her all the time.'

Inspector Rankin returned to the station and sent for WPC Kelly whom he knew as a caring person who had experience of rape victims. She came into Rankin's office and stood waiting for instructions.

'There's a nasty case of rape up at the hospital,' said Rankin.

'Oh dear,' murmured Kelly.

'I couldn't get a word out of her. Neither can the staff. See what you can do.'

'Right.'

WPC Kelly left the station and made directly for the hospital. She was shown into the victim's room.

'Hello,' she said, smiling warmly.

The girl just looked at her as she had looked at Rankin.

Kelly could see from the state of the girl that she had had a rough time. She had never seen anyone in such a bad state.

'We've got to find the bastard who did this to you,' she said. 'I could kill him myself when I look at you.'

Kelly took the girl's hand and held it in hers.

'What is your name, dear?' she asked.

'Barbara,' whispered the girl, hoarsely.

'Barbara. Where do you live, Barbara?'

There was no reply.

'Don't worry. Take your time.'

11

Kelly kept stroking the girl's hand.

'We can't do anything without your help, you know. You've been through the mill I can see, but I'm afraid it's not over yet. But everything will be done for your own good.'

The girl called Barbara looked scared.

'Don't be frightened. You're with friends.'

Barbara tried to smile but couldn't because of her injuries.

'Let me tell you what will happen,' began Kelly. 'I've got your medical record here from the Sister. Crushed windpipe. I can see the angry marks on your neck. What was he trying to do? Kill you? I'll kill him. I can see you've been punched in the face and you've got knife cuts on your thighs and tummy. He obviously tried to strangle you and no doubt thought he'd succeeded. He'll probably be surprised that you're still alive. Good for you, dear. He tried to kill you, didn't he?'

'Yes,' whispered Brenda.

'Looks like it. He's got a nice surprise coming to him if you can help us. Otherwise we'll never catch him. So this is what we want. A thorough examination by a sympathetic doctor is needed as soon as possible after the event. Which means now.'

'No. No,' croaked the girl.

'I know. You think you've been through enough but I promise you every probe and swab is vital. You shouldn't even have a bath yet. I'm sorry but human cells left in the attacker's body fluids could help to identify him. They deteriorate quickly so we have to act fast.'

Barbara looked aghast. Only half understanding.

'Now, don't be frightened, dear. We're all with you. I'm telling you these things in detail so you won't be shocked or upset. Three vaginal swabs are taken at varying depths. That shouldn't hurt you. They're cotton buds you've seen and they are swivelled at the entrance, halfway up and against the cervix. I'm sorry but it's got to be done or we're lost. We also take samples of your hair and saliva from your mouth. Even your fingernails are searched for traces of the bastard's skin in case you scratched him or clawed him in some way.'

Barbara was barely able to speak. She whispered her answers through her battered windpipe. She was obviously in pain each time she tried to speak, swallow, or move her neck.

'What I want you to do, Barbara, when you are able, is tell me as much about the man as you can so that if you saw him again...'

Barbara suddenly shuddered and croaked, 'No! No!'

'...if you saw him again you could say, "That's him." I know I'm asking a lot but without your help I'm lost. I keep saying that, I know, but I'm determined to nail this bastard. It's the worst damage I've seen inflicted on anyone so will you, please, let our doctor examine you?'

'If you stay with me,' croaked the girl.

'Yes,' said Kelly. 'I'll stay with you.'

Before any of that could happen WPC Kelly had to report back to Detective Inspector Rankin.

'I must say, Chief, that's the worst case I've come across.'

'Pretty bloody, isn't it?'

'The man obviously tried to kill her as well. Which means he could have another go when he knows she's alive.'

'In that case we can set a trap for him. Let the Press have the story but keep them away from her

13

and we'll put a twenty-four hour watch on her. A policeman outside her door.'

'She's prepared to be examined by our doctor. After a struggle.'

'Good. I'll set it in motion.'

'On consideration I stay with her.'

'Do you mind?'

'Do you mind, more like it.'

'There's nothing else you're on, is there?'

'No.'

'Then go back to her and find out all you can.'

'Right.'

WPC Kelly returned to the hospital.

'Hello, Barbara,' she cried. 'It's me again.'

Kelly got the impression that the girl was pleased to see her, though she was still curled up and shaking.

'Where do you live, Barbara?' Kelly asked.

Hesitating and with difficulty Barbara managed to recite her address. The effort at once exhausted her.

'Thank you, dear. We'll have the place watched.'

'Why?'

Kelly did not want to alert the girl to the possibility of the man coming back once he knew she was alive so she said, evenly, 'Our men will comb the place for clues.'

'He didn't come in.'

'Never mind. They may find something.'

The doctor arrived to conduct the examination.

'Hello, Kelly,' he said, recognising her from experience.

'Go easy with her, doctor.'

'Don't worry.'

'She wants me to stay. Hold her hand.'

'Good idea.'

As the doctor approached the bed Barbara cried out, 'Why can't I be left alone?'

'You promised,' said Kelly, taking her hand.

The examination proceeded slowly and gently. Every now and then the girl cried out, 'No! No! No!'

Ignoring the protestations, the doctor continued until at last the examination was completed. Barbara lay back and closed her eyes, tears coursing down her cheeks.

'You're a brave girl,' said the doctor.

'Thank you, dear,' said Kelly.

She stayed with the girl after the doctor had left.

'Well done, dear,' she repeated.

'Horrible,' the girl croaked.

'I know. It's all over now and with luck we'll learn something about the man.'

Inspector Rankin spoke to the editor of the local newspaper and told him what he wanted. Apart from a brief story about the vicious rape of a local girl, he did not want any reporters bothering her at the hospital.

Already detectives from the Bensham police station were out hunting. They contacted all the people in the neighbourhood where Barbara lived. Did they see anything? Did they hear anything? The answers were always in the negative.

WPC Kelly had gleaned a certain amount of information from Barbara through her calm persuasion. She passed the information on to Rankin.

'She tells me she was on her way back from the Saturday dance at the Corn Exchange when the man threatened her. He was chewing gum all the time and when he got excited he chewed faster. That's about all I can get out of her.'

'That's a help,' admitted Rankin. 'We'll put a notice in the papers inviting all the men who were at the dance to submit to DNA.'

'All of them?'

'They'll submit if only for elimination. Particularly the ones who danced with her.'

And so it transpired. All those men who were at the dance when Barbara was attacked offered themselves for testing. One of the men said, 'She danced with one man nearly all the time. It was quite noticeable.'

'Who was that?' asked Rankin.

'A chap called Harry Brook. We were all jealous.'

'He's been tested.'

After the testing Rankin was no nearer finding the rapist. The only news was that the girl's car had been found. It had been abandoned in a cul-de-sac not far from the girl's home. The car was immediately brought to the police station and Forensics went over it with a fine tooth comb. The first thing they noticed was an empty packet of chewing gum on the floor by the back seat. This tied up with Kelly's information gleaned from Barbara herself. It was obvious from the interior of the car that something terrible had taken place. The sun roof had been slashed with a knife and so, too, had the seat belts. All the windows were shattered. There was no blood in the car. There were fingerprints which were checked with all possible suspects but to no avail.

All this time Barbara was still in bed recovering from her wounds. WPC Kelly called to see her as often as possible. She had no other visitors because she had no relations. Her friends at the office and the tennis club steered clear because of the type of case it was.

Every time Kelly visited the hospital, however, she noticed that a man stood on the other side of the road. It was always the same man. He was well dressed, smart, good-looking, a gad-about Charley. He was always in the same position, just looking across at the hospital. Kelly became suspicious. Was it someone waiting to get near Barbara? Had he read that she was alive when he'd thought otherwise? Was it, in fact, the rapist? She felt that she was being ridiculous and letting her imagination get the better of her. She told Rankin of her suspicions. He sent a man to keep watch.

The detective watched from a distance. He noticed that the man hardly moved from his vantage point. He just stood there for hours on end. He did not move away until the darkness of the night set in. The detective followed him. He went into the nearest pub. The detective waited outside. He followed the man when he came out after about half-an-hour and then continued with him to his home, which was several streets away from Barbara's road but still in Bensham.

The detective reported to Inspector Rankin. Both men agreed that the man's behaviour was suspicious to say the least. Rankin decided to have him brought in for questioning.

Consequently the detective approached the man on the pavement opposite the hospital.

'Excuse me, sir,' said the detective. 'May I ask why you stand out here on the pavement so regularly?'

'Of course you may,' replied the man in a cultured accent.

There was a pause, the detective thinking the man would explain himself.

'Well?' prompted the detective.

'What do you want to know?'
'You've been here every day for the last two weeks.'
'That's right.'
'Why?'
'Do I need a reason?'
'Are you waiting for someone?'
'No.'
'Are you looking for someone?'
'No.'
'What are you doing here?'
'Just looking.'
'It seems highly suspicious.'
'Does it?'
'Would you mind coming down to the station and answering a few questions?'
'Not at all.'
'Follow me.'
The two men set off for Bensham police station and the man was shown into Inspector Rankin's office.
'Well,' said the man, 'now that we're here, what happens?'
'Let me put you in the picture, young man,' said Rankin, with some condescension. 'I am investigating a rather nasty case of rape with intent to kill.'
'So I heard.'
'You happen to live not far from the home of the girl involved. She happens to be in Bensham hospital at the moment where you seem to have been keeping some kind of vigil.'
'Yes.'
'Can you help us in any way?'
'How, for instance?'
'Fingerprints. DNA.'
'You mean you suspect me?'

18

'No. Just the process of elimination.'

'But I've been eliminated once.'

'You have?'

'Yes.'

'When?'

'I was among the dancers at the Corn Exchange that you called in.'

'You were?'

'I was the last person to dance with her.'

'You didn't see her home?'

'We had separate cars. We were going to meet next day at the cinema.'

'So that's you.'

'Better look at your records, Inspector.'

'I apologise. But you must admit your behaviour is unusual.'

'Not unusual to me.'

'You mean you're interested in her?'

'I'm not her boyfriend if that's what you're thinking.'

Rankin had been searching through his records.'

'You're Richard Connor,' he said.

'That's right. You've got it at last.'

'I can only apologise for misjudging you. But you must understand we have a hell of a job on our hands.'

'I don't envy you.'

'Where are you going now? Back to the hospital?'

'Probably.'

Rankin shook hands with the man and apologised once more but Mr Connor found it all rather amusing.

Once the man had left Rankin said, 'I appear to have a certain amount of egg on my face.'

'It doesn't show, sir,' said the detective.

'Get me WPC Kelly.'

'Yes, sir.'

When Kelly came into Rankin's office he said, 'This is a fine mess you got me into.'

'Me?'

'Your phantom suspect outside the hospital was the last person to dance with the victim.'

'I did notice that he didn't chew gum.'

'Chew gum?'

'Our man chewed gum all the time. He told the girl it was because he had a fear of bad breath when he kissed someone.'

'Luckily the man Connor took it in good part.'

'Thank God for that.'

'I'm going to have another look at that farm gate,' said Rankin, getting to his feet.

He assembled enough men to search the area around the farm gate, the lane and the meadow. They found an empty packet of chewing gum which they would pass on to Forensics.

Much to Rankin's surprise, he saw that Richard Connor was standing on the other side of the lane watching the progress. Why? How did he know they were going to the farm? In spite of the fact he had no record there was something strange about Mr Connor.

WPC Kelly was still keeping Barbara company at the hospital. The girl was still in a lot of pain and it would obviously take some months for her to recover completely, yet she managed to submit to the questioning and detail necessary for the artist to produce an identikit.

The identikit was reproduced in every newspaper in the county and Rankin, Kelly and all the others sat back and waited. Someone's bound to recognise the likeness and get in touch with them. So they thought. But there was absolutely no reaction whatsoever so Rankin was no further ahead in apprehending the rapist than he was at the beginning.

Months passed and nothing happened and Barbara was still in hospital. Mr Connor was still keeping a vigil outside. Barbara had greatly improved mentally and she was prepared to talk about her ordeal in more detail but she still suffered from the wound in her throat. The stab wounds were healing, too.

House-to-house enquiries were still taking place, with negative results. Rankin appealed to the public on the television and still nothing happened. He had never known anything like it. There was not even a slight chink in the rapist's armour. He must be somewhere. Someone must know him. He couldn't have vanished. Rankin felt that he was faced with an unsolved murder which frightened him. What would his boss say?

There was nothing for it but to search the records for years back in the hope that some similar idiosyncrasy might lead somewhere.

There was much groaning among the crew as Rankin spelt out his plan. It would mean hours of possibly fruitless searching among dusty files dating back years. Rankin decided that the period should be ten years. The decision did not make him popular. He called for any possible suspects with a similar *modus operandi* to the missing rapist. That is, knife to the throat, lounge suit, posh accent, chews gum.

The entire operation took ages, weeks, months. It was a mammoth task, causing not a few frayed tempers. Rankin was ridiculed and condemned for such a heartless upheaval.

One of his researchers, Detective Constable Evans,

had given up hope when he reached for the last file on his desk. It was dated exactly ten years ago. What a hope, he thought.

He glanced idly through the dossier. On the front was printed the name Ronald Haigh. The name meant nothing to him. Inside there was an identikit. There was something familiar about it. Where had he seen that face before? Then it clicked with him. Of course. It was the present case of the girl Barbara. It was just a likeness, nothing more. A lot of people probably looked like it. Wait a minute, though. What's this? Lounge suit, upper-class accent, chews gum. Evans read on, intrigued. The man had committed a series of attacks on women in their cars. Once he had raped a girl he drove away in her car and left it abandoned. The man wore a mask. Evans remembered something from Barbara's statement. 'I left my bloody mask behind.' Evans read that the man had been in prison and, according to the detective's calculations, was due out a couple of months ago. Problem: where was the man?

Detective Evans took the file to Rankin in his office.

'Take a look at that, Chief,' he said, handing him the file.

'What have you got there?'

Rankin looked at the file.

'Ten years old,' he mused. 'Ronald Haigh. Rings a bell.'

He opened the file and began to read the contents. Evans stood waiting.

'Sit down, man,' said Rankin.

Evans sat dutifully opposite the Inspector's desk.

Rankin compared the file of ten years ago with the one for the present day.

'Seems to fit, doesn't it?'

'I thought so,' admitted Evans.

'Where is this Ronald Haigh now?'

'The only address is ten years old.'

'Mm... We can only try.'

'Want me to go and see?'

'Better.'

'Right.'

Evans made a note of the address from the old file and set off in search of the elusive Ronald Haigh. Ten years was a long time to live in the same house, especially as some of that time was spent in prison. The road, he discovered, was parallel to Barbara's. Was that at all significant? Evans wondered.

He rang the bell of the terraced house. The door was opened by a rather large lady of something more than middle age looking quite belligerent. She obviously let rooms.

'Excuse me, madam,' said Evans, politely. 'Does a Mr Ronald Haigh live here?'

'Who wants to know?'

'I do.'

'Who are you?'

'Bensham police.'

Evans showed his badge.

'What do you want him for?'

'I'd like to ask him a few questions.'

'What sort of questions?'

'I'd rather deal with him, if you don't mind.'

'I'm his mother.'

'Oh.'

'Can't you people leave him alone. I know he was in trouble once. But that's all over. He's clean now.'

'I'd still like to talk to him.'

'Well, he's not in.'

'When will he be in?'

'I've no idea.'

'Where is he now?'

'At work.'

'Where's that?'

'He's one of the cashiers at the supermarket.'

'What time does he get back from there?'

''Bout six o'clock.'

'I'll come back then.'

'Please yourself.'

The lady shut the door. Evans began to walk away. As he did so he noticed that phantom character Richard Connor standing on the other side of the road. How did he get there? How did he know the police were interested in Ronald Haigh? Evans ignored the man and made his way to the supermarket to take a look at the suspect.

On entering the store he stood back to observe the line of cashiers at the checkout. They were mixed, male and female and Evans had no difficulty in picking out Ronald Haigh. He was smiling happily as he served the customers. He was obviously popular with everyone. He didn't look like a killer and, Evans noticed, he was surreptitiously chewing gum. Evans reported to Inspector Rankin.

'He's still there,' he explained. 'The house is owned by his mother. He works at the supermarket where I saw him in action. You wouldn't think that he had a care in the world. Incidentally, as I was leaving the house our phantom voyeur was standing on the other side of the road.

'What was he doing there?' asked Rankin.

'He seems to dog our footsteps.'

'If he's so interested in the girl I wonder he doesn't try to see her.'

'Perhaps he's tried. But no one can see her yet. She's not well enough.'

'Possible. Kelly says she's still in a bad way. I hope she's well enough to come to court.'

'There's plenty of time for that. She should be.'

'We'd better bring Haigh in.'

'I'm hoping to meet him at six.'

'Think he'll come quietly?'

'If he's still there. His mother is bound to warn him.'

'I'd like to search his room.'

'I can do that if I have a warrant.'

'I'll get one by then.'

'If he's not there I can still do a search.'

'If he's done a runner it proves his guilt.'

'I have an idea he'll brazen it out. He looks the type.'

'Go to it, Evans. And good luck.'

'Thank you, Chief.'

At six o'clock Evans rang the bell at the Haigh house. The large lady opened the door.

'It's all right,' she said. 'He hasn't run away.'

'Good,' replied Evans.

Evans stepped into the hall as the lady opened the door invitingly.

'Third floor back,' she said.

'Thank you.'

Evans climbed the stairs which at least were carpeted though somewhat threadbare. He knocked on the door of the room at the back of the house.

'Come in,' called a pleasant voice.

Evans entered a bed-sitting room that looked clean and well furnished.

'Mr Haigh?'

'That's me.'

'Detective Constable Evans.'

'Yes. Mother said you'd called. Can't think why?'

25

'We're making enquiries about a rape case.'

'Oh, no. I've been through all that and done my time but I'm clean now and I think you people should give me a chance and leave me alone.'

'You know the old story: no stone unturned.'

'I'm clean, I tell you. Ask my mother.'

'I have a warrant to search this room.'

'Whatever for?'

'That's what I hope to find out.'

Evans went to the door of the room, turned the key in the lock and put the key in his pocket.

'What are you doing that for?'

'In case you take it in your head to run away.'

'I'm not likely to do that.'

'Good. You just sit there while I have a look round.'

'You still haven't told me why you've picked on me.'

While Evans began to search the room, looking in drawers and cupboards he explained, 'The present rape case is similar to yours of ten years ago except that this one was more violent.'

'How do you mean, violent?'

'He tired to kill her. In fact, it's pretty obvious he thought he had.'

'I don't go in for violence.'

'Glad to hear it. This man is also well spoken, as you are, wears a lounge suit, as you do and chews gum, as you do.'

'Quite a coincidence.'

'That's what you call it?'

'It wouldn't stand up in court.'

'No?'

Evans had come to one of the chests of drawers and as he rummaged among the shirts he found a dark blue balaclava. He took it out and held it up.

'What's this?'

'Oh, that. I used it when I went to a fancy dress party last year.'

'Another coincidence?'

'You think what you like.'

'I think I'm taking you in, Mr Haigh.'

'In where?'

'To the station. To have a word with Inspector Rankin.'

'You mean you're arresting me?'

'I'm taking you in for questioning.'

Evans switched on his mobile phone and spoke to Bensham police station.

'Evans here. Give me Rankin.'

He waited. Then, 'Chief, I've got Haigh with me. I think you'll want to talk to him but I need a car to bring him in. Thank you.'

Evans switched his mobile off.

'Might as well put your feet up while we wait for the car,' he said

'You're making a great mistake, you know,' said Haigh. 'There'll be a hell of a row when my lawyer gets hold of it.'

'We're used to lawyers,' said Evans, complacently.

It did not take long for the car to arrive and Evans escorted Haigh down the stairs. Haigh's mother met them at the door.

'Where are you taking him?' she demanded.

'Don't worry, Mother,' said Haigh, giving her a kiss. 'It's all a mistake. I'll be back in a minute.'

Once they were in the car Haigh said, 'Poor old Ma. She worries about me.'

He was trying to make conversation because, in spite of his bland manner, he was very nervous.

Faced with Inspector Rankin he made his usual bleat, 'I don't know what you want me for.'

27

'We want you to help us with our enquiries,' said Rankin. 'We are faced with a case of rape and attempted murder.'

'Don't look at me.'

'Where were you on the night of July 24th?' asked Rankin.

'God knows. When was that?'

'A couple of months ago.'

'Watching TV, I expect. Such as it is.'

'I notice you chew gum.'

'Always have done.'

'Our assailant chews gum.'

'A lot of people do. Mr Wrigley would be out of business if they didn't.'

'Why do you?'

'I have a horror of halitosis.'

'So had our assailant.'

'Very commendable.'

'Do you know a place called Oldfield Farm?'

'Where's that?'

'Half an hour from here.'

'I expect I've passed it without knowing.'

'The girl was raped there. Whoever did it took her car and abandoned it. Just as you did some years ago.'

'Yes. I admit it. But I'm clean now.'

'We shall see. Are you prepared to submit to a DNA test?'

'Anything you like.'

'You don't object?'

'Of course not. I have nothing to hide.'

'Take him away, Evans, and do all the necessary.'

'Right,' said Evans.

Evans got up and called to Haigh, 'Come with me, Haigh.'

Haigh dutifully followed Evans out of the room. Rankin took up Haigh's file and studied it again. If the DNA proved positive he would charge the man with rape and intent to kill and the search for Barbara's assailant would come to an end.

In a matter of hours the tests undertaken by Haigh were conclusive. Rankin had him in his office and charged him with the offence.

'You can't do that!' protested Haigh.

'I can and I have,' said Rankin. 'Put him in a cell, Evans.'

Evans led Haigh away with some difficulty for he was struggling and protesting all the time. Rankin was elated. Everything pointed to Haigh as Barbara's assailant. Everything fitted. All he wanted to do now was organise an identity line-up and hope that Barbara would pick Haigh out. He sent for WPC Kelly to alert Barbara to the need for an identity parade.

As soon as she came into the room he said, 'We've got him!'

'Oh, good,' said Kelly.

He threw the file across the desk to her.

'Take a look. Everything fits.'

'Ronald Haigh,' mused Kelly, as she read the report.

'He's still saying he didn't do it but, as you can see, the whole thing fits him like a suit of clothes.'

Kelly handed back the file.

'Congratulations, sir,' she said.

'Evans did the donkey work,' admitted Rankin. 'But what I want you to do now is get in touch with Barbara and see if she'll come to an identity parade.'

'I'll try. But she's still very sick, you know.'

'It will only take a minute.'

'I'll have a go.'

'Good.'

When she arrived at Barbara's room at the hospital the ward sister warned her that Barbara was by no means cured. Some of her wounds had healed but she was still in a distressed state of mind. With such a warning in mind Kelly made her way to Barbara's room. She opened the door carefully, quietly and peeped into the room. Barbara was sitting up in bed supported by several pillows.

'Hello,' said Kelly.

'Who is it?' asked Barbara, shielding her eyes.

'WPC Kelly. Remember?'

'Oh, yes. Hello.'

Kelly sat on a chair beside the bed. She wanted to take Barbara's hand but felt that the girl didn't want her to.

'How are you, dear?' she asked.

'Oh, I don't know,' moaned Barbara. 'Sometimes I don't think I'll ever be right again.'

'Of course you will.'

'I still have terrible nightmares.'

'They'll go. In time.'

'You think so?'

'Well, dear, I have some news for you.'

'What's that?'

'We've found the man who did it to you.'

'You have?'

'Definitely.'

'Good. I hope he hangs.'

'So do I. But we can't do that.'

'Why not?'

'It's not allowed.'

'This shouldn't be allowed. What he did to me.'

'I agree. But he'll get his just deserts. Don't worry.

Every bit of evidence we've got points to him. There's only one thing left to clinch it.'

'What's that?'

'An identity parade.'

'What do you mean?'

'We line up half a dozen men and you pick out the one you recognise.'

'Oh, no!'

Barbara showed real fear again.

'No? Why not?'

'I couldn't do it.'

'He won't see you. You'll be behind a screen. They won't see you come or go. All you have to do is pick the man you recognise.'

'No. I'd rather not.'

'But Barbara...'

'No. Don't ask me.'

'We can't go on without you. Without your help the man will get away.'

'I don't want to see him again. Ever.'

'All our work will be wasted.'

Tears welled into Barbara's eyes.

'Don't you think I've been through enough? What with your doctors and everything? No! No! No! Go away!'

'I'm not going away because I want to help you. The only way I can do that is by pleading with you to help yourself. You owe it to yourself to put this man away. You're lucky to be alive. The next one may not be so lucky. I know it's expecting a lot. If he does it again and the girl dies you'll wish you'd picked him out.'

'But you've got him, you said.'

'We've got him and charged him but before we can get him to court...'

'Court?'

'Why, yes. We want him put away, don't we?'

'I couldn't stand up in court.'

'Not now, perhaps. But the court's a long way off. You'll feel better by then.'

'No.'

Kelly began to feel desperate. She saw an opportunity slipping through her fingers.

'All right,' she said. 'Let's forget about the court and all that. What about the identity parade?'

Barbara made no reply. They sat in silence. Kelly waited patiently.

'I'll think about it,' said Barbara, finally.

'That all?'

'I'm tired.'

Kelly realised that the time had come to leave.

'Just remember, dear,' she said, 'we can't go ahead without you.'

Barbara's reply was to close her eyes wearily.

When Kelly left the hospital she was amused to notice that the phantom Mr Connor was still standing opposite, watching and waiting.

She reported to Rankin, 'Not very helpful, I'm afraid, Chief,' she declared.

'Oh?'

'She's frightened.'

'Shit!'

'She had a pretty rough mauling.'

'I know, but...'

'She's still in a sorry state.'

'You told her no one would see her?'

'Of course.'

'We may be able to manage without her but the defence will push for mistaken identity and all the rest of it. It doesn't help the jury.'

32

'The fresh wounds have healed but she's a mess inside.'

'Has she seen a psychologist?'

'I believe so.'

'How did you leave it?'

'She said she would think about it. But I'm sure she said that to get rid of me.'

'Well, that's something.'

'I don't want to badger her.'

'Of course not.'

'Do you think you could get one of the nurses to talk to her?'

'I'll give it a little time.'

'Up to you.'

Barbara, in fact, was as worried as Rankin. She wanted to help the police because she wanted the man caught. She just did not want to be reminded of her ordeal. She had seen identity parades on television. People watched behind a glass screen that was obscure on one side. It would mean leaving the hospital for that period of time. She couldn't walk there. She could hardly walk at all at the moment. She couldn't even walk to a car. She would need a wheelchair. She would talk to the nurse about it.

'Oh, we can get you there all right,' said the nurse.

'I don't want to let them down,' declared Barbara.

'I hope they catch the bugger.'

'Oh, they've caught him.'

'Well then, you don't want him to get away.'

'I don't know how I'd feel if I saw him.'

'Angry, I should think,' suggested the nurse.

'Yes. That. But...'

'He can't hurt you any more. He won't see you. I've seen what happens.'

'You think I should go?'

'I think you should help the police.'

'How will I get there?'

'I'm sure the police would pick you up.'

'I can hardly walk.'

'We'll get you a wheelchair.'

'Will you?'

'Of course.'

WPC Kelly received a telephone call at Bensham police station.

'Miss Kelly?' asked a very small voice.

'WPC Kelly speaking.'

'This is Barbara.'

'Oh. Hello.'

'I've decided to help you.'

'Oh, good. Thank you.'

'I don't know how I'm going to get there. The hospital say they'll give me a wheelchair.'

'Don't worry, dear. We'll see to all that. I'll pick you up myself. And thank you again.'

The man whom the police called the Phantom Mr Connor was standing outside the hospital when the police car arrived to take Barbara to the identity parade. The collapsible wheelchair was stowed in the boot and Barbara was carefully helped into the car by WPC Kelly. Later, the same Mr Connor was standing outside the police station.

Barbara was so fearful of the forthcoming encounter that she had draped a scarf round her head so that only her eyes were showing. She was wheeled into the viewing area where half a dozen men of similar appearance were standing against a wall with numbers above their heads. With Barbara were WPC Kelly, Inspector Rankin and DC Evans.

The lights were switched on to reveal the suspects. Immediately Barbara let out a scream.

'That's him,' she cried, pointing to number five. 'Get me out of here. Quick!'

The girl became hysterical, tears running down her cheeks, banging the arms of the wheelchair with her fists. Kelly tried to pacify her.

'You're all right, dear,' she said. 'They can't see you.'

'I can't stand it. Get me out of here,' screamed Barbara.

Rankin tried to intervene.

'You definitely identify Number Five as your assailant?' he remarked.

Kelly could have killed her Chief for being so pompous and irritating at a time when he could see the girl was in great distress.

'Yes! Yes! Yes!' she cried, tearfully.

'I'll get you back, dear,' said Kelly wheeling the girl away from the scene. She was still wailing and moaning.

Rankin rubbed his hands gleefully as he turned to Evans.

'That clinches it!'

Kelly wheeled Barbara out of the police station and helped her into the car. She sat with her as they made their way back to hospital. The girl was still sobbing quietly. Kelly held her hand to comfort her. She helped her, with the aid of a nurse, to get back into bed where she lay exhausted.

'That was very brave of you, dear, and thank you,' said Kelly.

'I hated it,' muttered Barbara.

'I know you did. It's all over now.'

'Is it?'

'Oh, yes. He'll stand trial. You've seen the end of him.'

She refrained from any mention of court proceedings. In her present state of mind Barbara would not be able to stand up in court and answer questions or submit to cross-examination. Thankfully, that would be some way off, several months probably, by which time Barbara should have grown stronger. For the present Kelly would not bother her, preferring to leave her in peace. That is, if it could be called peace in her case.

Kelly reported back to Rankin.

'It will take some time for her to get over that,' she remarked.

'Never mind,' said Rankin. 'We got what we wanted.'

'At what cost to her?'

'I know it must have been a shock seeing the man again after all she suffered. I think you'd better continue to keep an eye on her.'

'I intend to.'

'We shall need her in court.'

'That's what worries me. The longer that can be put off, the better.'

'Have you mentioned it to her?'

'No. I daren't yet.'

'I must admit that bloody man did a lot of damage to her.'

'We've got him now, anyway.'

'Yes. And we're going to keep him.'

In fact, Ronald Haigh was committed for trial at Bensham Assizes. The prosecution had plenty of evidence against him, including some of the bloody and damaged underwear that was rescued from the girl after the rape. He was charged not only with rape but with wounding with intent to kill, as evidenced by her injuries. Rankin and Kelly were cock-a-hoop at their success and quite a show trial was anticipated.

* * *

Kelly kept in touch with Barbara and was happy with the girl's progress. She was getting stronger and her attitude and demeanour were improving. The question of appearing in court was still not mentioned. In any case, the date for the hearing was quite a few months ahead.

And then came the moment when Kelly actually brought up the question of a court appearance.

'I'm not going to court,' said Barbara, simply.

'What?' asked Kelly, aghast.

'I'm not going to court.'

'Not at all?'

'Not at all.'

'But...'

'No buts. I'm not going.'

'Why not?'

'I couldn't face it.'

'You're the chief witness. There's no case without you.'

'I don't care.'

'Barbara, you can't do this to us.'

'I've made up my mind.'

'Then the man will get away.'

'He can't. You've got him.'

'He has to stand trial.'

'I don't.'

'I don't know what to say.'

'Don't say anything.'

'Do you need more time? Is that it?'

'No. No matter what time it is. I stay here.'

'You can't be in hospital forever. There will come a time when the doctors say you can leave.'

'That won't be yet.'

'No. But…'

'Don't keep on.'

'I'm sorry. I'll have to go back to Inspector Rankin.'

'Do what you like. I'm going to sleep now.'

Barbara closed her eyes as a sign for Kelly to leave. Kelly hesitated. She wanted to pursue the problem but decided at last to return to Inspector Rankin.

'The girl seems to have taken over,' Kelly explained to the Inspector in his office.

'We can't make her appear,' said Rankin.

'Does that mean the case falls down?'

'Not necessarily. I'll get in touch with Counsel. She won't even make a screen appearance?'

'She won't do anything. It's a complete change around. She asked me to leave.'

'I thought she'd got over her hysterics after the identity parade.'

'She's not hysterical now. She appears to be in complete control.'

'And yet…'

'No doubt a psychologist could explain the sudden change.'

'Oh, yes. Reverse rationalisation process, I expect.'

'Do you want me to try again?'

'I think you should keep in touch.'

'She's not easy to talk to now.'

'Odd.'

'Incidentally, our phantom Mr Connor is still hanging about outside the hospital.'

'I don't think he can help us.'

Kelly went on her way and Rankin conferred to prosecuting Counsel.

Much to Rankin's surprise, Counsel for the prosecution was not at all put out by the possibility of the rape victim not appearing in court. There was enough evidence against Ronald Haigh to convict him a dozen times. No worry. So the case went ahead.

Kelly noticed that the Phantom Mr Connor was in the public gallery. There was the usual toing and froing in the court among the opposing lawyers. Ronald Haigh denied the charges and his Counsel contended that the identity parade was a case of mistaken identity. It was all circumstantial evidence as far as they were concerned. They only had Rankin's word for the fact that Barbara identified the man as Haigh. Although she signed a statement to the effect in a moment of hysteria she was not in court to verify the statement or physically identify the man in the dock, all of which the judge allowed as legitimate defence. To add insult to injury, the defence even suggested that Barbara was a willing participant in the sexual encounter.

Rankin could not believe his ears when he heard such blatant lying. He whispered as much to Prosecuting Counsel, who only smiled and said that was easily disposed of. Which he proceeded to do by showing photographs of Barbara, showing her face and neck where she had been beaten up and the stab wounds on her thighs and stomach. He then held up the girl's blood-stained and torn underwear.

'Is this the sign of a willing victim?' he asked.

At once Defence Counsel was on his feet protesting. The photographs, he contended, could be faked and as the so-called victim was not in court the suspected undergarments could not be verified. Such evidence, he persisted, should not be allowed.

Much to everyone's horror, the judge agreed with Defence Counsel's opinion. The case against Haigh was beginning to crumble. According to the judge, without the presence of Barbara the trial could not continue. It was the duty of the prosecution to produce the young lady. In the circumstances, the judge adjourned the trial until such time as the girl could be produced.

This created some consternation and WPC Kelly and Inspector Rankin called on Barbara in hospital trying to persuade her to attend Court.

'The judge has given us time to persuade you,' explained Rankin.

'You can't persuade me,' said Barbara. 'I've told you before. I've had enough.'

'Then the man will go free,' said Kelly.

'He will never go free,' said Barbara.

'How do you make that out?' asked Rankin.

'God will punish him.'

Shit, thought Kelly. We're on the religious tack now. She and Rankin exchanged significant glances. The girl's a bit deranged Kelly decided. We don't stand a chance.

Rankin tried his hardest to get the girl to change her mind but she was adamant and he and Kelly came away feeling utterly defeated. Neither of them said a word as they made their way back to Bensham police station.

As they went inside Kelly asked, 'Did you notice our Phantom Mr Connor outside the hospital?'

'No,' said Rankin, absently.

'He was in the public gallery in court as well.'

'Was he?'

'Wherever we go he's not far away.'

Kelly was making conversation. Rankin was not really interested in what she was saying.

So Ronald Haigh became a free man once more,

much to Rankin's disgust. He returned to his bed-sit in his mother's house. But he was no longer employed at the supermarket. After all the publicity they decided to dispense with his services. He spent part of his time writing to lawyers claiming damages for wrongful arrest.

It was a few days after Haigh's freedom that the police received an urgent call from his mother.

'Come quickly,' she cried. 'Ronald's hanged himself!'

Rankin and Evans hurried to the scene, alerting the ambulance on the way. A sobbing mother led them upstairs to Ronald's room where they found him hanging from the ceiling light.

'Is he...?' cried his mother.

'I'm afraid so,' said Rankin, having tested the man's pulse.

'You go downstairs, Mother,' said Evans. 'Leave it to us.'

She went out of the room sobbing audibly.

'That's funny,' said Rankin, musing.

'What is?' asked Evans.

'I don't think he did this himself.'

He was examining the hanging material very carefully. The hanging material, he noticed, was not rope or cord but piano wire affixed to the ceiling socket.

'If you wanted to hang yourself, Evans, would you use piano wire?' asked Rankin.

'If I couldn't find anything else, I suppose,' replied Evans.

'It makes strangulation last longer.'

'I didn't know that.'

'Look at the way it's fixed round his neck and onto the ceiling. He couldn't have done that himself. Someone's kicked the wooden chair away but not

41

this chap. He's also been hit in the face. See? He didn't do that himself.'

'I'd better ask the mother if anybody's been in.'

'No. Wait. We might as well treat it as suicide. After all, we don't owe him anything.'

'That's true.'

'You could call it just deserts. I think we'll leave it, don't you?'

'As you say, Chief.'

By the time the Inspector had made his decision the ambulance people had arrived to deal with the body and he and Evans returned to the police station.

As they left the terrace house they noticed the Phantom Mr Connor standing on the other side of the road. He was grinning broadly and as he saw Inspector Rankin he gave him the thumbs up sign. Rankin and Evans stopped in their tracks and stood aghast.

'Do you think he could have...?' began Rankin Then, suddenly, 'No. Forget it.'

He walked to the hospital and this time he went inside. He asked to see Barbara. The receptionist said, 'I believe there's someone with her. Hold on.'

She pressed the button on her phone.

'Constable,' she said, 'there's a Mr Connor who wants to see Miss Hammond.'

'Send him up,' replied WPC Kelly.

She sat by Barbara's bed and waited for the visitor to arrive. He came into the room and stood at the bottom of the bed.

'Hello,' he said.

The girl looked up in surprise.

'We were going to the cinema. Remember?' he said.

'So we were,' replied Barbara.

Then Kelly noticed an extraordinary thing. Barbara smiled for the first time.

MURDER AT THE ABBEY

According to the guide book, Rockerby Abbey was situated in Buckinghamshire within 20 miles of London. It was one of those vast piles open to the public where the family who had owned the place for hundreds of years lived in a small apartment in some corner out of the way on the first floor. It was of historic interest, of course, with ornate, decorative ceilings, antique furniture and paintings and all the rest of the paraphernalia that people paid money to gaze at with envy or admiration. In addition to the Abbey itself, with its extensive grounds and large, ornamental lake, there were the usual safari park attractions, complete with wild animals of all sorts and a fun fair with a scenic railway, big wheel and dodgems.

Without such commercialism the family could not live. As it was, they were not exactly affluent. There was a time, years ago, when the old duke was alive, when money was no object and the old boy even had the railway line diverted to what became known as Abbey Halt so that he could get to London more easily. What with inheritance tax and one thing and another, the remaining members of the family were economically crippled.

Only three of them now lived in the Abbey; the latest duchess, an elderly widow who still thought she owned the place and acted accordingly; Lady Pamela, her daughter, tall, dark, unmarried and likely to remain so, and her son, Lord Newton, known to the family as Freddy but to the staff and others as Golden Boy because he was a very good-looking blond young man who spent a good deal of his time chasing the wrong type of girls, according to his mother. All the time she and his sister were urging him to marry someone of their own kind he was

45

dallying with shop girls, the Abbey maids or any susceptible visitor who thronged the place on open days. As he was the last of the line they were anxious that he should produce an heir, otherwise the family would become extinct. Eligible members of the opposite sex did not appeal to him. He did not want a permanent relationship or commitment.

In spite of his dalliances, Freddy made himself useful on the estate and was particularly interested in the safari park, showing more concern for the animals than he did for his mother's choice of partner. He went to London on occasions when he would stay at his club. He had a few male friends, mainly left over from university, otherwise he was a bit of a loner. His mother, the duchess, called it laziness. If Freddy would only marry and take over the Abbey then she and her daughter were prepared to move into one of the dower houses on the estate. The odd thing about the family was that Pamela herself had no wish to marry and in that respect was not unlike her brother. Lady Pamela was more interested in good causes. She was entitled to wear the uniform of the St John's Ambulance Brigade, an outfit that suited her well.

All of which was the great concern of the duchess, faced as she was with the prospect of a son and daughter becoming a bachelor on the one hand and a spinster on the other. She complained about it to everyone she met and the gossip columns of the newspapers were inclined to refer to them as the still unmarried Lord Newton and Lady Pamela. Since they were both in their late thirties, the speculation was perhaps reasonable.

Apart from that, the family was not famous in any way. They were a normal, noble family. Newspaper editors were inclined to dismiss them, even tiring of any mention of the eligibility of the one known as Golden Boy. It wasn't worth the bother of printing. They were not to know that in the not too far distant future the family would be front-page news, not mere gossip, due to the murder of a nondescript girl who happened to be visiting when the Abbey was open to the public.

Apart from Freddy's interest in the safari park, the fun fair and the food hall, he also supervised the public visitors when the Abbey was open, keeping an eye on the queues and making sure that certain rooms remained private.

It was this privacy that caused the trouble. It was a day in June and the visiting period as far as the visitors were concerned was at an end. They had either driven away in their cars or made their way to Abbey Halt, which was within walking distance.

Freddy was making his customary tour of the rooms to make sure that everything was in order. He went into one of the private bedrooms and discovered a young girl there.

'Hullo,' he said. 'What are you doing here?'

'Just looking,' replied the girl.

She was an attractive creature, which Freddy was not slow to appreciate. He looked her up and down, noting her nubile figure.

'The visit's over,' he told her. 'Didn't you hear the bell?'

'No.'

'You know this is a private area.'

'Oh. Is it?'

'As if you didn't know.'

'I didn't. But I did wonder why there was no one else here,' explained the girl.

'I could have you arrested for trespassing. You've read the rules on the board by the gates.'

'No. I didn't read them. I just followed the others from the train.'

'You came by train?'

'Yes.'

'You've missed it now. There won't be another one for a couple of hours.'

'Oh, lord.'

'Where do you live?'

'Brampton.'

'Where's that?'

'North London. I'm sorry I intruded. I didn't mean to. I'll go.'

'Just a minute.'

Freddy approached the girl and put his hand to her face, gently. He pulled her towards him.

'Now, wait a minute,' the girl cried in alarm.

'What for? We're in a bedroom. We might as well make use of it.'

He took her face in his hands and kissed her greedily on the lips. She struggled to free herself but he held her fast and then threw her onto the bed.

'You're trespassing,' he stormed.

The girl tried to get up and run away but he pushed her back on the bed. He put his hand up her skirt.

'No! No! Stop it!' she cried.

After pawing and mauling the girl, Freddy proceeded to rape her. In spite of her hitting him with her fists and crying out for help, he managed to penetrate her. When he stood up she was lying on the bed in floods of tears, her dress dishevelled.

'Don't be a bloody fool,' said Freddy. 'That wasn't new to you.'

'You're a horrid beast,' she sobbed.

'Come on,' commanded Freddy. 'Dress yourself and get out.'

'I'm going,' she moaned.

Once she had straightened her clothes and adjusted her make-up she went out of the room. She hesitated at the door.

'Which way is it?'

'I'll show you.'

Freddy led the way down the stairs to the front door, opened it and let her out without a word. She hurried away, half walking, half running.

Freddy's sister, Lady Penelope, saw him shutting the door.

'Who was that?' she asked.

'Some kid who got lost. I found her in one of the private rooms.'

'I hope you ticked her off.'

'I certainly did.'

Lady Pamela was as dark as her brother was fair. She had shiny black hair without a wave in it. She wasn't particularly attractive. People said she was straight up and down, which she was.

As they walked away together Pamela said, 'If that goes on we'll have to put more wardens round the place.'

'Oh, I don't think she had any ulterior motive. She just got lost.'

The girl in question, whose name was Janet Harvey, made her way to the Abbey Halt station. The stationmaster, who was also the porter and ticket collector, nodded to the girl as she entered the station.

'You been to the Abbey?' he asked.

49

'Yes.'

'Did you get left behind?'

'Sort of.'

'All the other visitors have gone. There isn't another train for over an hour.'

'I can wait.'

The stationmaster was used to the comings and goings of visitors to the Abbey. One minute there was nobody in the station and the next there would be a sudden rush on the days when the Abbey was open to the public. Then there was another rush when the visit was over. While Janet Harvey was waiting he chatted to her.

'Wonderful place,' he said.

'Yes.'

'The ceilings. Did you see those?'

'Yes.'

'Did you see the animals?'

'No.'

'Worth a visit. Sometimes you can hear the lions roaring from here.'

'Really.'

'Nice family.'

'Yes.'

Although she answered in the affirmative, she had reservations, bearing in mind her recent experience. The stationmaster wanted to chat but Janet wanted to be left alone. He told her how long he'd been doing the job, how many people get off the train to visit the Abbey, how the station came to be so near the Abbey, how the old duke had the line diverted years ago, how he'd turn up in a pony and trap to join the train.

Janet was relieved when the train arrived. The stationmaster opened the door for her and saw her off. She watched the countryside fly by as the train took her to her home town of Brampton where she lived in a semi-detached house with her mother and father. The town, north of London, was known as a garden city because someone decided to plant trees either side of the road. At least, that was the opinion of Janet's father, a retired employee of the town hall and a bit of a busy-body.

'Did you have a nice day, dear?' asked her mother as Janet came into the sitting room on her arrival back from the Abbey.

'If you can call being raped by his lordship a nice day, yes,' Janet replied.

'What!' exclaimed Father, who was sitting in an armchair on the other side of the fireplace from his wife.

Janet sat down and explained how she had wandered inadvertently into one of the wrong rooms in the Abbey and how Lord Newton had accused her of trespassing and how he had raped her on the bed and sent her packing.

'How awful!' cried Mother.

'We'll see about that,' threatened Father, getting up from his chair.

'What are you going to do?' asked Janet, fearfully.

'Get on to the police, of course.'

Father was about to go out of the room to the telephone in the hall when Janet stopped him.

'No, Father,' she begged. 'Don't do that.'

'Why not?'

'I don't want to go through all that publicity business. You know what it's like. You've seen it in the papers. It's so embarrassing. Let me deal with it.'

'How?' insisted Father. 'How are you going to do that? He shouldn't be allowed to get away with it.'

'Let me see what happens,' said Janet.

'What do you mean? You told us what happened.'

'Let me see if I get pregnant.'

Father turned to his wife in some confusion.

'What do you say, Mother?' he asked.

'Let Janet do it her way.'

'That's all very well,' he protested.

'If anything happens,' continued Janet, 'then I'll write to him and ask him to contribute to the support of the child.'

'He'll tell you to go to the Welfare,' suggested Father.

'If he does, then I'll go to the police.'

'I don't like the gap in between,' complained Father. 'It weakens the case.'

'When will you know, dear?' asked Mother.

'In a couple of weeks.'

Father slumped down in his armchair, reluctantly.

'Bastard!' he exclaimed.

When Janet realised that, without a doubt, she was pregnant she told her parents. She said she was going to write to Lord Newton and ask him what he intended to do.

'He won't marry you. You know that,' said Mother. 'People don't today.'

'I know that, Mother,' declared Janet, 'but he can contribute towards the maintenance.'

'Take a copy of the letter you write,' advised Father, who didn't trust anybody and remembered what a useful habit it was from his experience in the town hall. Always keep a record was his dictum.

'Do you want it, Janet?' asked Mother.

'Want what? The money?'

'No. The baby.'

'Of course I want it. Don't you?' ·

'We're going to be grandparents,' she declared to her husband.

'Can't say I'm excited about that,' Father moaned. 'In the circumstances.'

'You will be when it happens,' concluded Mother.

Janet wrote her letter to Lord Newton and showed it to her father for approval.

'You haven't mentioned money,' said Father.

'Should I?'

'Of course. Otherwise he'll just dismiss it.'

'All right. I'll do it again.'

'Take a copy.'

'I will.'

'Then we'll see what the bastard has to say,' remarked Father, gloatingly.

Janet posted the letter herself at the nearby letter box, making sure that there was sufficient postage on the envelope.

Nothing happened. The letter was delivered to the Abbey. Freddy opened it among the rest of his mail, read it and promptly tore it up, thinking no more about it. He recalled the incident but decided it was not worth bothering about. It was nothing new to him and he dismissed it from his mind.

Janet waited a few days before worrying.

'I've had no reply to my letter,' she told her father.

'He should have answered by now,' said Father. 'He can't be all that busy. After all, what does he do?'

'Perhaps he's going to ignore it,' suggested Mother.

'We'll give him to the end of the week,' decided Father.

'What then?' asked Janet. 'Not the police.'

'No. I suggest you write to the duchess herself, his mother, with a copy of your original letter. And this time you send it recorded delivery.'

'That's an idea!' enthused Mother.

'What do I say to the duchess?' asked Janet.

'Tell her what happened, just as you told us. And enclose a copy of your letter to him. You can do that, can't you?'

'Of course.'

'Shouldn't we threaten to tell the police?' asked Mother.

'Yes,' said Father.

'I don't want the police involved,' complained Janet.

'No,' agreed Father, 'but you can hint at it. To frighten them. If they don't cough up. You could say something like before I go to the police I feel I should put you in the picture. So on and so on.'

'I see,' said Janet, dubiously.

Janet made several attempts to write the final letter, tearing them up as she went along, until she was satisfied with it. She showed it to her father for approval and this time walked to the local post office to record the special delivery.

Then she waited.

At the Abbey there was no way of avoiding the delivery of the letter and when the duchess read it she was sitting in their small drawing room with her daughter, Lady Pamela.

'Christ all bloody mighty!' screamed the duchess, suddenly.

'Mother!' cried Pamela. 'Whatever is it?'

The duchess thrust the letter towards her daughter. 'Read that.'

Pamela took the letter and read it.

'I don't believe it,' she said, quietly.

'Where's Freddy?' demanded the duchess.

'I don't know,' admitted Pamela.

'Find him. Get him on the mobile and tell him to come here at once.'

'The mobile's in my room. I'll get it.'

Pamela hurried out of the room.

'Bloody fool,' muttered the duchess to herself.

When Pamela returned, having made the phone call, she asked her mother, 'What are you going to do?'

'I don't know. I'll have to speak to Freddy first. Where was he?'

'In the amusement park.'

'Typical.'

'There must be some logical explanation. I can't believe...'

'The logical explanation, my dear, is obvious. Freddy's been up to his tricks again and seems to have picked on the wrong one. One that's determined to be difficult.'

'Why can't he leave them alone?'

'Because he's a randy bastard. We'll see what he has to say.'

At that moment Freddy burst into the room.

'What's the panic, Ma?' he asked.

'Read that,' demanded the duchess, holding out the offending letter.

'What's this?' he asked, taking the letter.

When he had finished he simply said, 'Oh.'

'Did you receive a letter from this girl?' the duchess asked.

'Yes.'

'What did you do with it?'

'I tore it up.'

'Why?

'I thought it sounded like blackmail. She wanted money, obviously.'

'Is there any substance in her claim?' asked Pamela.

'Substance? My God, Pam. You trying to act the lawyer?'

'Did you rape her?' asked the duchess.

'No.'

'But you had sexual intercourse with her.'

'Yes. She seemed willing.'

'Another one of those,' commented Pamela.

'She was trespassing,' protested Freddy. 'I found her prowling about in one of the private bedrooms.'

'Ah!' exclaimed Pamela. 'You saw her out of the front door. I remember.'

'That's no excuse to rape her,' said the duchess.

'It wasn't rape.'

'She says it was.'

'She's a liar.'

'If she can prove it was against her will it's rape.'

'How can she prove that?'

'It's her word against yours.'

'And which one do you believe?'

'It's not for me to believe, dear. You can see she's thinking of going to the police.'

'Bluff.'

'The point is,' decided the duchess, 'what do we do about the veiled threat?'

'Threat?' echoed Freddy. ' She won't do anything.'

'Why didn't you see her and pay her off, Freddy, when she first wrote? That would have been the end of it. Instead of which she goes to the trouble of sending a letter by recorded delivery which can't be ignored.'

'Why not?' asked Freddy.

'Do you realise what would happen if she went to the police?' asked the duchess. 'Rape is a serious offence.'

'If proved.'

'Are you prepared to go through with all the publicity, blood tests of her child and all the rest of it? Do you realise what a field day the newspapers would have?'

'What am I supposed to do? Marry the bitch?'

'No one's suggesting that,' retorted Pamela.

'I'll have to see her,' said the duchess, glumly.

'She's only after money,' insisted Freddy.

'I can't risk ignoring her.'

'Are you thinking of paying her, Mother?' asked Pamela.

'It might be worth it.'

'What? A hundred pounds?'

'She's more likely thinking in thousands,' said Freddy.

'Then she's got another think coming,' declared the duchess. 'In fact, I'll get her to sign an agreement.'

'That's a good idea,' said Pamela.

'Then it's agreed,' concluded the duchess. 'I write to this creature and invite her to come and see me.'

'On your own head be it,' commented Freddy.

'It's for your sake I'm doing it, Freddy,' said the duchess.

'Thank you, Ma. Do you want me any more?' he asked.

'No. You can go.'

Freddy strode out of the room.

'That boy!' muttered Pamela.

During the day the duchess wrote a very guarded and formal letter to Janet Harvey inviting her to the

Abbey to discuss her problem. She mentioned a time of four o'clock in the afternoon.

In the Harvey household there was jubilation when Janet showed the duchess's letter to her parents.

'Well done, dear,' said Mother.

'That's more like it,' added Father. 'Do you want me to come with you?'

'No, Dad. Thank you. I can manage.'

'Don't let them get you down.'

'I won't.'

'Don't let their titles faze you.'

'I won't.'

'They must be worth a few thousand.'

Janet dressed carefully for the journey to the Abbey, not that she had that an extensive wardrobe to choose from. She was determined not to give the impression of anything but a demure young lady. She was seen off by her mother and father who wished her good luck and waved from the front gate until she was out of sight. It was the last that they would see of her alive.

At Abbey Halt, the stationmaster expressed surprise when he saw Janet alight from the train.

'You back?' he asked, recognising the girl. 'It's not open today.'

'I know,' said Janet.

The man watched her walk away towards the Abbey, a lone figure, lost in the vast area of the landscape with its long path from the ornamental gates to the house. It was four o'clock in the afternoon and there was not a sound in the air, not even a bird singing.

Janet was slightly breathless when she pulled the great iron bell at the front door. It was opened by

Fletcher, the butler, though she was unaware of his name. He looked at her as if she shouldn't be there.

'I have an appointment with the Duchess of Rockerby,' declared Janet.

'Name?'

'Janet Harvey.'

'Oh, yes.'

Fletcher had been advised by the duchess that the girl was expected. He opened half of the huge door and invited her inside.

'This way,' he directed.

He led the way across the hall to a drawing room on the first floor where the duchess was waiting, standing in the middle of the room.

He knocked on the door and when he heard a voice say 'Come in' he opened it and announced, 'Miss Harvey,' your grace.

Janet entered the room and Fletcher closed the door behind her.

'Good afternoon, your grace,' said Janet, nervously.

'Sit down,' commanded the duchess, coldly, still standing in the middle of the room.

Janet sat down carefully on the edge of one of the upright chairs. The duchess looked her up and down imperiously.

'First of all, Miss Harvey, I must tell you that my son denies everything that you say in your letter.'

'Well, he would, wouldn't he?' said Janet.

'Are you suggesting that he is a liar?'

'I know what happened and so does he.'

'What are you after? Money?'

'I'm pregnant, as I told you in my letter. As I told your son.'

'Doesn't the Welfare or whatever it's called, deal with that?'

'Basically, yes. I suppose so. But it's very little.'

'So it is money you're after.'

'I'm only asking for ordinary maintenance.'

'You intend to keep the child?'

'Oh, yes.'

'Why?'

'Because it's alive.'

'Well, Miss Harvey, I'm here to tell you that you'll get nothing out of us.'

'Did you invite me all this way to tell me that?'

'Yes.'

'Your son raped me and made me pregnant and you're not prepared to do anything about it?'

'Nothing.'

The duchess had changed her mind about even the offer of one hundred pounds. She could ill afford it and she turned against the girl suddenly, considering her common.

'We'll see about that,' said Janet threateningly. She stood up.

'You're very sure of yourself,' accused the duchess.

'Very. Because I know what happened.'

'What proof have you?'

'It's inside me.'

'I don't believe that's anything to do with my son.'

'There are ways of telling who's the father these days. The police usually deal with it and I intend to let them know what happened. Good afternoon, your grace, or should I say disgrace.'

She turned and made for the door.

The duchess was so angry and infuriated that she hurried after the girl, grabbing a heavy candlestick on the way.

'Come back here, you little slut,' she cried.

She lifted up her arm and with her full force hit

the girl on the back of the head with the candlestick. The girl fell down heavily.

'Get up, you stupid cow!' growled the duchess.

But the girl did not move. The duchess pushed her with her foot but she still did not move. The duchess stood horrified.

She hurried to the door and called out, 'Pamela!'

Her daughter came running from her own room because of the urgency of the cry. She had, in fact, been awaiting the result of her mother's interview.

As she stepped into the room she asked, 'What's the matter?'

Pamela stopped short as she saw the prostrate figure of the girl on the floor.

'What happened?'

'I hit her,' said the duchess.

'I expect she's only unconscious.'

Pamela's knowledge of first aid helped her to establish the condition of the girl.

'No, she's not,' she said.

'What?'

'She's dead.'

'Oh, God.'

The duchess slumped into a chair.

'What did you hit her for?'

'She made me angry. She was going to the police.'

The duchess still held the candlestick in her hand. Pamela calmly took it away from her and put it back on the table.

'I'd better tell the police what I've done,' muttered the duchess.

'For God's sake, no! Hang on. I'll get Freddy.'

'Where is he?'

'I don't know. I'll get him.'

She went out of the room to find her mobile

telephone and returned with it to the duchess. She pressed the digits and waited.

'Freddy? Where are you?'

She listened to the reply.

'Never mind about that,' said Pamela, curtly. 'Get here as quick as you can. Something terrible has happened.'

Evidently Freddy wanted to ask questions but Pamela cut him short.

'Get here!' she commanded, cutting the phone off.

'I didn't mean to kill her,' moaned the duchess from her chair. 'I wanted to stop her getting away. She was going to the police. Imagine! Accusing Freddy of rape.'

'I'm afraid I wouldn't put anything past him,' admitted Pamela.

'How can you say that about your brother?' admonished the duchess.

'I have no illusions as far as he's concerned.'

When Freddy came into the room he was breathless from running. He stopped suddenly when he saw the body of the girl on the floor.

'Shit!' he exclaimed.

He looked closely at the body and turned to his mother.

'That's the girl,' he said. 'The one...'

'Yes, Freddy. We know,' said the duchess. 'The problem now is what to do about it. I wanted to tell the police but Pamela says no.'

'Quite right,' agreed Freddy. 'What happened?'

'She threatened to go to the police accusing you of rape...'

'Yes. But how did this happen?' persisted Freddy.

'I hit her with a candlestick.'

'Killing her.'

'I didn't intend to. I just wanted to stop her. I didn't know how.'

'I thought you were going to buy her off,' said Freddy.

'It wouldn't have been the end. She was on about maintenance. That would have gone on and on. We can't afford it and on top of that I didn't like her.'

There was a silence between the three of them. Freddy paced about the body while Pamela stood by her mother's chair watching.

'What do we do?' she asked.

'Who knows she's here?' asked Freddy, thoughtfully.

'Only Fletcher,' replied the duchess. 'He let her in.'

'Right,' said Freddy. 'First of all we'll hide her. Wrap her up in a rug and hide her in the cupboard. Then we'll wait until dark and get rid of her.'

'And how do you propose to do that?' asked Pamela.

'Where does she live? I've forgotten.'

The duchess consulted the girl's letter.

'Brampton,' she said.

'Good. We put her in the Land Rover and drive her to Brampton or somewhere near. Somewhere where's there a wood and dump her. That'd give the impression that she was killed there.'

'Brilliant,' said Pamela.

'What do you think, Ma?' asked Freddy.

'I can't think. I'm still shocked.'

'Never mind. We'll deal with it. Won't we, Pamela?'

'Of course. You'll need someone to help you with the body,' said Pamela.

'Yes. I was going to ask you.'

'I'll help you, of course.'

'Thanks.'

'I don't know how you're going to do it,' complained

the duchess. 'With all these people about the place. Fletcher and the rest.'

'We'll make sure they're all asleep,' explained Freddy. 'We don't want anyone to see the car driving away.'

'Fletcher will wonder when the girl's leaving,' said the duchess. 'He'll expect to let her out.'

'You can tell him you let her out, Ma,' suggested Freddy.

'Yes. As I invited her it would make sense,' said the duchess.

'In the meantime,' declared Freddy, 'we'd better get rid of the candlestick.'

'Why?' protested the duchess. 'It's valuable.'

'Not as valuable as your life, Ma,' said Freddy. 'It's got blood on it plus your fingerprints.'

'What does that matter?' asked the duchess. 'No one's going to see it.'

'Better be on the safe side,' insisted Freddy.

'What do you mean?'

'What are you afraid of?' put in Pamela. 'If we dump the body at Brampton the police won't come looking here.'

'I'd be happier to throw the candlestick in the lake,' said Freddy. 'Remember, the girl has a letter from Ma. Someone may want to know when she left here because she'll be missing, won't she?'

'My poor candlestick,' moaned the duchess.

'Won't the staff notice it's missing?' asked Pamela.

'If they do I'll say I've sent it to London to be valued,' said the duchess.

'Good idea,' agreed Freddy.

So it was arranged that Janet's body was wrapped in a car rug and kept in a cupboard in the duchess's room until Freddy and Pamela were ready to remove it. The candlestick was likewise wrapped up in cellophane and put with the body until it was dark enough for Freddy to throw it in the lake.

At dinner that evening the duchess ate heartily but Freddy and Pamela did not appear to be very hungry. They, of course, were anxious about the macabre task awaiting them. It would not be dark until quite late as it was summertime. The duchess, however, appeared to have lost her fear of retribution and basked in the confidence of Freddy and Pamela who, she felt sure, would solve her problems. She seemed to have forgotten that she had killed a young girl whose body was still in her apartment. She was once more the imperious Duchess of Rockerby.

Later in the evening Freddy and Pamela held a whispered conversation in the drawing room while the duchess was dozing off after dinner.

'I'm afraid we're in for a long wait,' said Freddy. 'We don't want anyone to hear us driving away.'

'Wouldn't it be more natural if you went now?' asked Pamela.

'It would if we didn't have to carry a body downstairs.'

'We could leave the car at the front door instead of getting it out of the garage. That would be a start.'

'No, some stupid sod is bound to ask if we wanted it put away.'

'Tell him no.'

'Then he'll wait up until I come back and move it later. You know what they're like. No, thank you. What we'll do when they're all asleep is push the car out of the garage. I won't start it up until we're out the front. I don't want some light sleeper telling the police he heard a car going out late.'

'The police?'

65

'Yes. It's possible. They could come snooping. What time did the girl get here? What time did she leave? That sort of thing.'

'But if the body's at Brampton...'

'This was still her last call and if she's missing someone is going to try to trace her last movements. I'm for playing safe.'

'I see. Yes. You're right.'

'We can't leave until after midnight.'

'What about coming back?'

'What about it?'

'They'll hear us. It'll be daylight. Early morning staff will be about.'

'Then we say we've been to a party.'

'I know!' exclaimed Pamela, suddenly. 'We'll dress. You wear a dinner jacket and I'll wear a gown and anyone who happens to be about when we get back can see we've been to a party.'

'Good idea,' agreed Freddy, enthusiastically. 'I'll change now.'

'So will I.'

Brother and sister parted to go to their own bedrooms where they would change their clothes. If Pamela's lady's maid asked why she wasn't called to help she'll say it was a last-minute decision. A midnight party.'

Just after midnight Freddy and Pamela made their way to the back of the building where the cars were garaged. Freddy opened the double doors quietly, got into the Range Rover and released the handbrake. Between them they pushed it out of the way so that they could close the doors. They then pushed the vehicle out of the way of any window. When they decided that the coast was clear they got in and drove to the front door. They hurried indoors and up the stairs to the duchess's room.

'Let me get rid of the candlestick first, Pam. Then we'll carry her out.'

He took the candlestick and hurried down the stairs again. When he came back he said, 'That's done. Now.'

He and Pamela went to the cupboard where the dead girl was propped against the wall. Together they carried her down the stairs to the hall. They had left the front door open purposely so that they could load the body into the car without any impediment. Freddy closed the front door as quickly and quietly as possible, which was not easy because it was so heavy.

With the body in a car rug they set off for Brampton. They didn't talk at all during the journey until they were nearing their destination.

'We'll aim for the station,' said Freddy. 'She came by train so she should have gone back there.'

'Try and find some open ground,' suggested Pamela, 'where she could have been attacked.'

They cruised slowly round the outskirts of the town until they came to an open space which was more like a rubbish tip.

'This'll do,' cried Freddy. 'Quick!'

Pamela scrambled out of the car hurriedly and moved with Freddy to the wide door at the back of the car.

'Don't slam the door,' warned Freddy.

The body was lifted out of the car and deposited on the open ground. Freddy pulled the rug away, which caused the body to roll over. He put the rug in the car and shut the door quietly. They both hurried to their seats and drove away.

'Phew!' breathed Freddy, once they were out of the town.

'Poor kid,' said Pamela.

'Poor kid?' queried Freddy.

'She looked so pathetic when you pulled the rug away and she rolled over.'

'We couldn't leave the rug there.'

'Of course not.'

'Ma will be relieved.'

'I'm sure she will.'

If Freddy had driven into Brampton itself he would have noticed that one semi-detached house still had its lights on, late that it was. It was Janet's mother and father staying up and wondering when their daughter was coming home.

By the time the brother and sister reached the Abbey it was quite light. Freddy stopped the car outside the front door and rang the bell.

'I didn't think of having to open the door again,' cursed Freddy.

'There's bound to be someone about at this hour,' said Pamela. 'Thank God we dressed up.'

The door was opened by Fletcher.

'I'm sorry, my lord,' he said. 'I didn't know you were out.'

'Last-minute party,' answered Freddy, breezily as he went indoors.

'Yes, my lord.'

Freddy and Pamela went upstairs together. They made for the duchess's room.

'Don't wake her,' said Pamela.

'I must.'

Freddy opened the bedroom door and went in. Pamela followed reluctantly.

'Wake up, Ma,' said Freddy.

The duchess opened her eyes sleepily.

'What is it?' she asked.

'We're back,' explained Freddy. 'We've done it.'

'Oh,' moaned the duchess, uncertainly.

'You know what we're talking about, don't you, Mother?' prompted Pamela.

'Yes. The girl.'

'That's right,' said Freddy. 'The girl.'

'You're in the clear, Mother,' said Pamela. 'You won't hear any more from her.'

'Thank you, dear. Thank you, Freddy.'

As Freddy and Pamela were going out of the room the duchess called, 'What are you doing dressed up?'

Freddy went up to the bed and whispered, 'To put Fletcher and the others off. We made out we'd been to a midnight party. Because it's daylight, you see.'

'I see. Very clever.'

'All part of the service, Ma,' declared Freddy as he went out of the room with Pamela.

'I'm going to bed,' said Pamela.

'So am I.'

True to Lord Newton's prophesy, nothing more was heard of Janet Harvey of Brampton. Nothing was heard of her at home, either. Mother and Father had expected her back from her visit to the Abbey at least by late evening, but when she hadn't returned by midnight they became worried.

'Perhaps she stayed the night,' suggested Mother.

'She'd have phoned us,' said Father

'The duchess's letter was quite friendly. She may have invited her to stay.'

'I've a good mind to phone the Abbey,' threatened Father.

'You can't at this hour.'

'I'm not frightened of them.'

'Neither am I. But it's after midnight.'

'I'll wait up,' said Father. 'You go to bed.'

'No. I'll wait up with you.'

They had settled in their respective armchairs either side of the fireplace to await the arrival of their daughter who never came. That is when Freddy and Pamela would have noticed the only house in the street with all the lights on if they had driven past. The worried parents only slept fitfully and at the time when Freddy and Pamela were arriving back at the Abbey, Mother made a pot of tea.

As he sipped his tea Father said, 'I don't like this. I'm going to ring the police in the morning.'

'It's morning now.'

'I mean later.'

He didn't ring the police, he called at the station himself. He knew them all very well round there. He spoke to the man at the desk.

'Hello, Joe,' said the policeman. 'What are you doing here?'

'My daughter. She's missing.'

'Oh, dear. Another one.'

'What do you mean, another one?'

'Kids. They're always running off.'

'She didn't run off. She went to visit Rockerby Abbey yesterday afternoon and hasn't come back.'

'Rockerby Abbey? Is there a pop festival on there or something, then?'

'No. No.'

'Only you know what some of these girls get up to.'

'My daughter had an appointment there. It was quite straightforward.'

'All I can do is put out a missing person notice,' explained the policeman. 'Details of height, age, colour and so on.'

'Is that all you can do?'

'At the moment. Have you phoned the Abbey to know when she left?'

'No.'

'It's an idea.'

'I'll do it when I get back.'

'Good luck.'

'Thanks.'

Father left the police station feeling more frustrated than ever. That policeman obviously thought that his daughter was just another tearaway.

He repeated the conversation when he got home and his wife said:, 'Oh dear. I'm afraid something terrible has happened.'

'I'm going to ring the Abbey,' said Father.

He looked for the letter that the duchess had written to his daughter. He took it into the hall where the telephone was situated at the bottom of the stairs. Mother followed him to hear what was said. Father dialled the number and a male voice, obviously Fletcher, the butler, answered:

'Oh,' said Father. 'I'm sorry to trouble you. Could you tell me what time Janet Harvey left yesterday?'

'Who?'

'Janet Harvey. She had an appointment with the duchess yesterday afternoon.'

'Oh, yes,' said Fletcher. 'I remember. I don't know what time she left. She didn't stay long I don't think.'

'She's not still there, is she?'

'Good Heavens, no!'

'Only she hasn't arrived home.'

'I'm sorry. I can't help you.'

'Thanks all the same.'

Father put the phone down and stood with his hand resting on it.

71

'She's not there.'

'I didn't think she was,' admitted Mother.

'What can have happened?'

'I'm going back to the police and tell them she's not there.'

He went out of the front door in a hurried, determined manner and Mother shut the door after him.

It was a different policeman at the station desk but the answer was the same. So Father returned home with the same news.

'It's not knowing,' moaned Mother.

Father called at the station every day and every day he got the same answer and every day Mother asked what could have happened. Until one day when a man was walking his dog near the waste ground outside the town. He came across the body of a girl. The dog barked furiously and the man hurried away to the police station to report his find.

Suddenly everything started happening. Tapes were slung round the area where the body was discovered, photographs were taken. The body was moved and the police surgeon undertook the work of examination. He pronounced that the girl had been killed by a blow to the head with a blunt instrument and that, in addition, she was pregnant. The body was then passed to the forensic department. In the girl's handbag was a photograph of herself, her name and address and a return ticket from Abbey Halt, unused.

In charge of the murder investigation was Detective Inspector Rankin, a middle-aged man with a military bearing in keeping with his neat, pencil moustache. It was his task to interview and question the girl's parents in Baring Road.

Father was sitting in his armchair reading the

morning paper before making his customary visit to the police station. Mother was busy in the kitchen. The front door bell rang.

'Someone at the door,' called Father.

'I can't go. I'm busy,' called Mother.

Father threw his paper down and heaved himself out of his chair. He opened the front door.

'Yes?' he asked, sourly. 'What is it?'

Inspector Rankin stood there.

'Mr Harvey?'

'Yes.'

'I'm Detective Inspector Rankin. I have news of your daughter.'

Father's demeanour changed immediately.

'Oh, good,' he cried. 'Come in.'

Father opened the door to allow Inspector Rankin into the hall.

'Come through,' he said, leading the way into the sitting room. 'Sit down.' He called out to his wife, 'It's about Janet, Mother!'

Mother hurried from the kitchen to join Father. She was wiping her hands on her apron.

'This is Detective Inspector Rankin, Mother,' explained Father.

'How do you do?' said Mother.

'It's not good news, I'm afraid,' said Rankin.

'Oh?' queried Father.

'Oh, no!' moaned Mother.

'Your daughter was found in a corner of the recreation ground.'

'She's dead!' cried Mother, collapsing into an armchair, holding a tea towel to her face.

'Someone has killed her with a blunt instrument on the back of her head.'

'Murdered?' cried Father. 'Why?'

'Oh, God,' moaned Mother, tears running down her cheek.

'She went to Rockerby Abbey and never returned,' said Father. 'Now we know why.'

'What was she doing there?' asked Rankin.

'It's a long story,' admitted Father.

'Never mind. I think I should hear it.'

Father turned to his wife solicitously.

'Why don't you go and lie down, dear?'

'No,' said Mother. 'I want to know.'

'Well,' said Father, addressing the detective. 'She went there on one of their open days. She often did that. Visit stately homes. This time, evidently, she had some trouble with Lord Newton and when she came home she said he'd raped her.'

'What!' exclaimed Rankin.

'Yes,' Father went on. 'He attacked her in one of the rooms she shouldn't have been in. She'd got lost.'

'The beast,' murmured Mother to herself.

'When she realised she was pregnant she wrote to him to ask what he was going to do about it,' continued Father.

'I expect Lord Newton was frightened of blackmail,' suggested Rankin.

'Not at all,' contradicted Father. 'She was only asking for normal maintenance.'

'Did Lord Newton reply to your daughter's letter?' asked Rankin.

'No,' said Father. 'So I suggested she wrote to the duchess, his mother, with a copy of the letter she'd sent to Lord Newton.'

'Did she reply?'

'Yes. She replied inviting Janet to call on her at the Abbey to discuss the problem.'

'That was something,' said Rankin.

'Janet went there at the time she was told but never came back.'

'What time was the appointment?'

'Four o'clock.'

'So it would still have been light when she got back here.'

'Yes.'

'She went by train.'

'Yes.'

'You're not far from the station so you would expect her to walk in this direction. Instead of which she was found in the opposite direction.'

'Who could have done such a thing?' asked Mother, from her armchair.

'According to Forensics,' explained Rankin, 'she had been wrapped in a car rug that was no longer there.'

'What does that mean?' asked Father.

'It suggests that she was killed somewhere else and dumped here.'

'What can have happened?' asked Mother. 'She would have been on the train.'

'There's some doubt about that. The return ticket was still in her purse.'

'Someone must have waylaid her,' said Father.

'Did she have a boyfriend?' asked Rankin.

'Not that we know of,' said Mother.

'Had she rejected someone who could have sought revenge?'

'Good Heavens, no!' cried Mother. 'She kept herself to herself.'

'The letters,' suggested Rankin. 'Have you got them?'

'Yes,' said Father. 'Here.'

Father went to the bureau that stood under the

window. He took out the letters and handed them to the detective. Rankin read the letters and made exclamatory whistling noises as he read.

'This is damaging stuff,' he declared. 'She's threatening to go to the police with a charge of rape.'

'That's right,' said Mother. 'When she got back from the Abbey she told us she'd wandered away from the public area and found herself in a bedroom that was out of bounds. She didn't know. Until this Lord Newton found her and said she was trespassing. Then he attacked her. She even told us what he said. "Might as well make use of the room," he said.'

'She told you all that?' asked Rankin.

'Of course,' confirmed Mother. 'She was upset. She said he raped her against her will. By the time she left the Abbey the rest of the public had gone and she made her way to the station alone.'

'I take it she didn't write to Lord Newton until she discovered that she was pregnant?' said Rankin.

'Of course not,' insisted Mother. 'I don't think she would have bothered otherwise. She wasn't asking him to marry her or anything. Just the maintenance.'

'As I say, that could be interpreted as blackmail,' said Rankin.

'She's still dead, isn't she?' accused Father. 'It's up to you to find the murderer instead of accusing our daughter of blackmail.'

'I'm not accusing her, Mr Harvey, but it's significant that Lord Newton should ignore her letter yet the duchess replied with an invitation.'

'To avoid a scandal, I expect,' suggested Mother. 'Because Janet hinted at the police. That must have frightened her.'

Rankin stood up.

'Well, thank you for all your help.'

'What happens now?' asked Father, also standing up.

'I'll try to find the murderer,' said Rankin. 'May I take these letters?'

'Yes. But I want them back.'

'I'll have them copied and return them to you. Oh, by the way, I'd like a photograph of your daughter to show people. Have you got one?'

'Yes,' said Mother. 'Here.'

She took a framed photograph from the mantelpiece and handed it to the detective.

'I'll also have it copied and returned to you.'

'Thank you.'

Then Mother asked, 'Can we see her? Can we see Janet?'

'Of course,' said Rankin. 'You know where the mortuary is?'

'I do,' said Father.

'When can we go?'

'When you like.'

'We'll go this afternoon, eh, Father?'

'Yes.'

'I'll let you know what progress I make,' said Rankin, as he made his way out of the door.

'Please,' said Father, escorting the detective to the front door.

When he returned Mother had resumed her work in the kitchen where he joined her.

'I hope they can do something,' he said.

'Whatever they do won't bring her back,' moaned Mother.

That afternoon they visited the local mortuary. Father made his way boldly. He'd been there before during his period in office at the town hall. Mother was more hesitant, frightened. They were shown their daughter's body by the attendant.

'Oh, God!' cried Mother. 'Janet!'

She was about to embrace the dead body when the attendant checked her.

'You can't touch her,' he said.

'Why not?'

'Forensics are still working on it.'

'Can't we take her home?'

'When Forensics have finished, yes.'

'When's that?'

'We'll let you know.'

Mother did all the talking. Father was grimly silent.

'We'll want to give her a proper funeral.'

'Of course. I understand.'

'You'll let us know.'

'Yes. We've got your number.'

'Come on, Father,' Mother concluded. 'I've seen enough.'

She led the way out of the building, Father following meekly, silently.

Inspector Rankin called at the local railway station where he showed Janet's photograph to some of the staff, all of whom recognised her.

'Her father used to work in the town hall,' said one.

'Did she buy a ticket to Rockerby Abbey recently?' asked Rankin.

'Yes,' said someone else. 'Twice.'

'Twice?' queried Rankin.

'Yes,' continued the man. 'Once when it was Open Day and later on when it wasn't.'

'You saw her each time?'

'Yes.'

'You saw her come back?'

'Yes.'

'Each time?'

'No. Only the first time.'

Rankin's mind went to the unused return ticket that was found in Janet's purse. In spite of that he continued to ask questions.

'Did anyone see her return the second time?'

They all shook their heads. Rankin thanked them and left. So, he mused, if Janet did not come back to her own station, as the ticket in her purse indicated, something must have happened to her even before Abbey Halt. That means that someone must have approached her in the Abbey grounds. To that end he decided to pay a visit to the station that served the Abbey and ask the people there if they recognised Janet Harvey and try to find out if anyone approached her on the way to the station. He would travel to and fro by train as she was supposed to have done. He did not intend to visit the Abbey itself. That was something he did not relish. He knew the type that occupied such places and did not look forward to the inevitable confrontation.

As the train travelled on, stopping at every station, Rankin was the only one who got out at Abbey Halt. He was in no hurry. He entered the station and gave his ticket to the station attendant.

'Nice day,' said Rankin.

'Makes a change,' muttered the attendant.

'Is it always as quiet as this?'

'It is if there's no Open Day at the Abbey.'

'Ah! I see.'

'It's a bit of a crush then. In and out.'

'I expect so.'

Rankin produced the photograph of Janet Harvey. 'Have you seen this girl before?' he asked.

79

'The man studied the picture.

'Something familiar about her,' he said. 'Can't think what.'

'She came here not long ago with the usual crowd.'

'Did she?'

'She may have been late in leaving.'

'That's it!'

'What?'

'She didn't leave with the crowd. She left later on her own and had to wait for the next train. That's right. We stopped and chatted.'

'Did she seem agitated at all?'

'No, wouldn't say that.'

'Then she came again, didn't she? Not on an Open Day.'

'That's right. So she did.'

'She went to the Abbey on her own.'

'That's right, yes.'

'Did you see her come back?'

'No.'

'You're sure of that?'

'Positive. Not while I was here, anyway.'

'What time do you go?'

'Quite late.'

'Thank you.'

Rankin moved away.

'Anything wrong?' asked the attendant.

'No. No.'

Rankin did not want to start any rumours.

'What time's the next train?' he asked.

'Over an hour yet.'

'I'll have a wander round, then, and come back.'

'The Abbey's not open.'

'I know.'

He left the station and started off towards the

ornate gates at the entrance to the Abbey drive, which appeared to be endless.

The station attendant was waiting when Rankin returned from his wandering.

'See what you wanted?' he asked.

'Yes, thank you.'

'Fantastic gates, aren't they?'

'They certainly are.'

'By the way, are you a policeman? You got that girl's picture, I mean.'

'I'm a detective inspector,' admitted Rankin.

'What's this about, then? Something to do with the girl?'

'Her parents are worried. She hasn't been home.'

Rankin did not intend to tell the man the whole story.

'That's nothing these days,' scoffed the attendant. 'It happens all the time. No discipline. That's the trouble.'

'You're probably right.'

'Some of the tales I hear. I tell you ...'

Abbey Halt was such a quiet, out-of-the-way station, except during Opens Days at the stately home, that the attendant was keen to chat with anyone who would listen to him. He was obviously intrigued that a detective should be asking about one of his visitors. Rankin found himself having to be non-committal in his replies as the man began to probe and gossip. He knew, though, that the time would come when it would be necessary to visit the Abbey in his official capacity.

Without Rankin's investigation, however, the cat was well and truly among the pigeons within the Abbey when the national newspapers published the story from the *Brampton Advertiser* of the murder of Janet Harvey with a photograph of the girl. Lord Newton saw the story first. He was sitting casually in the family drawing room enjoying his morning coffee and reading the newspaper. Pamela came into the room to join him. Suddenly the calm was broken as Freddy jumped up from his chair clutching the paper in his hands.

'Christ!' he cried.

'What?' asked Pamela. 'What is it?'

'Look at that!'

Freddy thrust the paper at his sister.

'Better keep it away from Ma,' he muttered.

Pamela read the story and handed the paper back to her brother.

'It doesn't mean anything to us,' she said.

'Doesn't mean anything?' echoed Freddy. 'It says she wasn't killed there but taken there from somewhere else. That means us.'

'No, it doesn't. We're in the clear. We covered our tracks. There's nothing to point to us. How can there be?'

'Yes. I suppose you're right,' said Freddy, somewhat mollified.

'Don't worry about it.'

Inspector Rankin was careful not to let the newspaper people know anything about Janet's visit to the Abbey. He did not want them nosing about in that quarter before he'd had time to investigate on his own. As far as they were concerned the girl's body was moved from the place of the actual murder to her own location. The venue of the murder could not be revealed but obviously, wherever it took place, the murderer knew where she lived and took the body home with the object of disguising the original venue. Among the people who knew where she lived were, of course, the Abbey family, as Rankin termed them.

He couldn't put it off any longer. He had to call at the Abbey. Before he did that he had a meeting with his superintendent with whom he had kept in touch throughout the investigation.

'The time has come for me to visit the Abbey, I'm afraid,' he said.

'On your own?' asked the chief.

'To start with.'

'I can see that lot raising hell in high places.'

'I'll have to risk that. Frankly, I don't think they carry a lot of weight these days. No matter what they might have been in the past, they're regarded as minor aristocracy today.'

'You're convinced the trail starts there?'

'Quite convinced. At least I might find out what time she left them.'

'Will you need to contact family members?'

'Lord Newton certainly. You've seen the letters.'

'Yes.'

'I'll have a chat with some of the staff if I can. The stationmaster there is sure the girl didn't leave by train.'

'Someone could have given her a lift.'

'That's what I would like to find out.'

'You don't need any warrants or anything?'

'Not at the moment.'

'Well, good hunting.'

'Thank you.'

Avoiding the tedious train journey and the walk to the Abbey, Rankin drove himself from Brampton in his own car. The ornamental gates were open, as they always seemed to be. As he drove on towards the building he was conscious of a sense of pride and poverty hovering over the place. Ignoring the various parking signs and directions, he made for the front door. He got out of the car and turned to look back at the vast acreage of park and lake that faced him. He turned again and rang the huge bell pull beside the front door. He waited. The door was eventually opened by the butler, Fletcher.

'Yes?' he asked.

'I would like to speak to Lord Newton,' said Rankin.

'Who wants him?'

Rankin showed his card.

'Police.'

'If it's a donation...' began Fletcher.

'I need to ask Lord Newton some questions regarding a certain event,' insisted Rankin.

'Oh,' said Fletcher. 'Come in.'

He opened the door wider so that Rankin could enter the hall.

'If you wait here I'll see if his lordship is available,' said Fletcher.

Rankin watched as the portentous gentleman climbed the wide staircase to some rooms upstairs.

Freddy and Pamela were together in the drawing room. They had just finished drinking their coffee when Fletcher knocked on the door.

'Come in,' called Freddy.

Fletcher stood in the doorway.

'Excuse me, my lord,' he said. 'There's a policeman downstairs asking to see you.'

'You know what to do. You don't have to bother me. If the man wants a bloody donation give him something.'

'He's a detective inspector, my lord.'

'Oh, is he? Did he ask for me in particular?'

'Yes, m'lord.'

'Bring him up them,' said Freddy.

When Fletcher had left the room Pamela moved to sit with her brother on the sofa. She patted his thigh.

'Take it easy,' she urged. 'Don't panic.'

'Don't worry. I'll play it by ear.'

Freddy may have appeared calm but Pamela could tell that he was nervous.

Inspector Rankin was shown into the drawing room announced by Fletcher who went out at once and closed the door.

'Detective Inspector?' queried Freddy. 'Where do you come from? I thought I knew all the police round here.'

'Brampton CID,' said Rankin.

'Brampton? You're a bit off your beat, aren't you?'

He had no intention of introducing his sister or asking the man to sit down.

'I'm investigating a murder that took place in Brampton,' Rankin explained.

'Then why come to us?'

'Because the girl concerned was last known to have come here.'

'My dear man,' declared Freddy. 'On Open Day thousands of girls come through these gates. I daresay some of them come from ... where was it? ... Brampton?'

'This one came on a day that was not Open Day.'

'Oh? That's odd.'

Rankin produced the photograph of Janet Harvey and handed it to Lord Newton.

'That's the girl,' he said.

Freddy took the photograph and studied it. He passed it to Pamela.

'Mean anything to you, Pam?' he asked.

Pamela also studied the photograph. Rankin stood patiently waiting.

'No,' said Pamela, returning the photograph to her brother who handed it back to the inspector.

'Can't help you, I'm afraid,' decided Freddy.

'In that case,' Rankin went on, 'perhaps this will help you.'

He took from his pocket copies of the letters he had been given by Janet's father. He proffered them to Freddy who took them gingerly. He began to read them.

'Oh. Her,' he said.

He passed the letters to Pamela.

'What do you say happened to her?' asked Freddy.

'She was murdered,' explained Rankin. 'Hit on the head with a blunt instrument.'

'Who would want to do that?' asked Pamela.

'That's what I hope to find out,' said Rankin.

'But why here?' asked Freddy.

'As you can see by the letters,' said Rankin, 'she was invited here by your mother.'

'Well?'

'She never left here.'

'How can you be sure of that? You said she was murdered at Brampton.'

'The man at the Abbey Halt station remembers her arriving on the train but not leaving.'

'She could have got a lift.'

'All the way to Brampton?'

'Possible.'

'There are plenty of men on the estate who would be only too delighted,' put in Pamela.

Rankin stretched himself to his full height.

'I would like to talk to her grace, if that's possible,' he declared.

'Why?' asked Freddy.

'She was obviously the last person to see the girl.'

'I suppose you're entitled to ask all these questions,' said Freddy.

'Quite entitled. Any refusal could be considered perverting the course of justice.'

'I don't think she'll be much help to you,' advised Freddy.

'We can only see,' said Rankin.

Freddy turned to his sister with a look that he hoped was a sign of warning.

'Will you see if Ma's about, Pam?'

'Sure.'

Pamela got up and went out of the room.

'I remember the girl now,' said Freddy, confidentially. 'Quite a piece.'

'She accused you of rape,' Rankin pointed out.

'Mere blackmail,' declared Freddy, dismissively. 'As a matter of fact when I found her in one of the private bedrooms I said we might as well make use of it while we're here and she didn't object.'

'Did she have a chance?'

'Of course she did. They all have. I'm not an idiot, Inspector. I know the signs.'

Rankin found it difficult not to voice his loathing for such a vain, conceited, smirking individual.

'She also accuses you of making her pregnant,' observed Rankin.

'That's easily dealt with.'

'Would you be prepared to go through with all the publicity of a pregnancy test?'

'What publicity?'

'You are a well-known person, a member of the aristocracy, as it's called. Don't you imagine the press would be interested in such a thing? At present I've purposely avoided letting them know the girl's last destination, which was this house.'

'Why should that bother them?'

'It wouldn't bother them but it might bother you.'

'How?'

'Would you want a lot of newsmen and photographers swarming all over the estate?'

'They wouldn't get very far. We have a very efficient security service.'

'That wouldn't stop them writing anything or taking photographs.'

'In our business, you get used to it.'

Rankin was amazed at the sheer cold-blooded attitude of the man. It was a kind of divine right that the man had. He found it infuriating but was unable to say so.

At that moment the door opened and the duchess came into the room accompanied by her daughter. She was at her most imperious; tall, formidable, not to be trifled with. She ignored the presence of Inspector Rankin.

'What's the trouble, Freddy?' she demanded.

Freddy indicated Rankin without saying a word.

'Who are you?' asked the duchess, rudely.

'Detective Inspector Rankin, your grace,' said Rankin.

'What are you doing here?'

'Investigating the last moments of a girl who has been murdered.'

'What's that got to do with us?'

In reply Rankin handed the duchess the photograph of Janet Harvey.

'Do you remember this girl?' he asked.

The duchess looked at the photograph with disdain.

'No,' she answered.

'Perhaps this will remind you,' said Rankin.

Rankin showed the duchess a copy of her own letter inviting the girl to the Abbey.

'Oh,' said the duchess. 'Her.'

'You remember her now?'

'Of course.'

'She came here to see you but did you see her leave?'

'She left me. I expect Fletcher saw her out.'

'Fletcher?'

'The butler,' explained Freddy. 'He brought you up here.'

'Could I have a word with him?'

'You don't object, do you, Ma?' asked Freddy.

'I don't object. But why is it necessary?'

'The girl never arrived home,' said Rankin.

'Surely that's not unusual these days?' suggested the duchess.

'She was murdered somewhere on the way.'

'Oh dear. That's bad,' concluded the duchess.

Rankin felt uncomfortable in the sudden silence. It was obvious to him that these so-called aristocrats had no intention of helping him.

'Well,' he ventured. 'I won't keep you good people any longer. If I have your permission to talk to some of your staff...'

'Help yourself,' said Freddy.

'Thank you.'

Rankin gave a little bow and went out of the room.

At once the duchess went to the door to listen and make sure that the detective had gone. Then she hurried to Freddy and whispered: 'Do you think he knows anything?'

'No,' boasted Freddy, expansively.

'What a creep,' cried Pamela. She mimicked the man. 'I won't keep you good people any longer.'

'What does he think he'll learn from the staff?' asked the duchess.

'He has to ask questions,' explained Freddy. 'It's all they can do.'

'It's the answers I'm worried about,' admitted the duchess.

'Don't worry, Ma,' assured Freddy. 'You're in the clear.'

On his way downstairs Inspector Rankin encountered Fletcher.

'Oh, Mr Fletcher,' he said. 'Could I have a word with you?'

'By all means, Inspector,' replied Fletcher, genially.

Once more Rankin produced the photograph of Janet Harvey.

'Have you seen...?'

Before Rankin could continue any further the butler interrupted him.

'We'd better go into my room,' he said.

Fletcher led the way to the staff quarters of the Abbey where he invited Rankin to sit at a large, square, plain wooden table in the middle of a large room with chairs and armchairs and where other members of the staff, mostly female, were coming and going.

'It's about that girl, is it?' asked Fletcher.

'Yes,' said Rankin.

'I know her grace invited her here because I wasn't going to let her in until she showed me the letter she'd got.'

'She got here, yes. Did you see her leave?'

'No.'

'Would you normally have opened the door for her?'

'Oh, yes. But her grace could have let her out herself.'

'Is that likely?'

'Well, no. Not really. But the girl could have slipped out herself. You could tell she wasn't used to having doors opened for her.'

'She never returned to the station. Abbey Halt.'

'She didn't?'

'According to the station attendant.'

'Someone could have given her a lift.'

'Who?'

'Anyone on the estate on their way home. She was an attractive girl.'

'Anyone on the estate? That's a wide net.'

'Yes. What with the safari boys and the fairground lot.'

'It wouldn't have been Lord Newton?'

'Good Heavens, no! He would think that beneath him.'

'You know what's happened, do you?'

'No. But I can guess.'

'Let me show you some letters. It's all right. They're no longer private property.'

Rankin produced the incriminating letters that he carried with him. He handed them to Fletcher who took some time reading them. When he returned them to the inspector he simply said, 'I'm not surprised.'

'Is there anyone else among the staff who might have seen the girl?'

'No. Her grace was anxious that the girl should be taken to her room straight away. Smuggled almost.'

'Isn't there someone about all the time? Dusting, hoovering, that sort of thing. In a large place like this.'

'Bless you, no. Once that work's done with they keep out of the way unless they're called.'

'Forensics say she was killed away from her own home and wrapped in a car rug that was no longer there.'

'It couldn't have been anyone here.'

'Why not?'

'Why would anyone move her from here to her own home? That is, if she was killed here. Which is not likely.'

'The only people who knew where she lived are her grace and her son.'

'She would have told anyone who gave her a lift where she lived.'

'Do you think the safari people and the fairground staff carry rugs in their cars?'

'I wouldn't have thought so.'

'Neither would I.'

'I suppose she had a return ticket.'

'Oh, yes. The unused half was found in her purse.'

'They don't always collect them at the station. Old Joe there gives up if there's a crowd.'

'Has anyone here been driving out late at night?'

'Driving out?'

'With a body in the car.'

'Good Heavens!' exclaimed Fletcher in alarm. 'Is that what you're thinking?'

'I'm thinking of everything and nothing,' admitted Rankin. 'Something must have happened to the girl near here. She never arrived at the sation. She's dumped at home in a car rug. By someone. For what reason? It's a puzzle.'

'I can understand your dilemma, Inspector,' conceded Fletcher. 'The only people who have been out late in the past few days are his lordship and his sister. They went to a midnight party and didn't come home until early morning. In fact, I met them as I came downstairs first thing.'

'Where was the party?'

'No idea. They were all dressed up.'

'Is there any way of finding out?'

'Only by asking them. Which I'm not prepared to do. I'm afraid you've got your work cut out, Inspector. I wish I could help.'

'Thank you anyway, Mr Fletcher. I'll get on my way.'

As Rankin got up to leave the door opened suddenly and a middle-aged woman in domestic uniform came into the room.

'I say, Fletch!' she cried, expecting to find him alone. She stopped in her tracks. 'Oh, I'm sorry,' she went on, 'I thought you were alone.'

Fletcher stood up and introduced her.

'This is Detective Inspector Ranking. Ivy Jason.'

'Oh dear,' moaned Ivy. 'What's Golden Boy been up to now?'

'Golden Boy?' queried Rankin.

'That's what they call Lord Newton,' explained Fletcher.

'Did you see Janet Harvey here, Ivy?' asked Rankin.

'Who?'

Fletcher stepped in to explain again.

'The girl you saw in the paper, Ivy. She was last seen around here.'

'I saw something in the paper about a girl who was murdered,' admitted Ivy. 'But I didn't read it all. But it wasn't here. I forget where it said she was found.'

'The inspector says she was killed somewhere else and left near her home. Her last known visit was here,' said Fletcher.

'I know Golden Boy gets up to all sorts of capers,' admitted Ivy, 'but I don't think he'd kill anyone. He hasn't got the guts.'

She turned to Fletcher.

'I see the old girl's flogged another candlestick. She says she takes them to London to be valued but they never come back. She's always carting off bits and pieces.'

'What kind of candlestick?' asked Rankin.

'One of those big, heavy, ornamental things. Ugly, I think they are. I'm not sorry to see it go. It's a bugger to clean.'

'When did you notice it missing, Miss Jason?'

'Oh, a few days ago,' she said, airily.

'You can't remember exactly?'

'Bless me, no! It happens all the time. They're always selling bits off. They have to keep it secret from the trustees.'

'What do you know about the trustees?'

'What everybody else knows. You can't avoid gossip in a place like this. We do our work because we're paid. We don't have to love 'em.'

'Any help, Inspector?'

'Afraid not,' admitted Rankin. 'Where do they usually sell things?'

'Lazenby's in Cork Street, London.'

'Thank you.'

When Rankin had left Ivy turned to Fletcher.

'What was all that about?' she asked.

'I told you. You saw about the girl in the papers. She was murdered in waste ground near her home.'

'What's that got to do with this place?'

'She was last seen calling here.'

'One of the crowd?'

'No. She was one of them one day but she wandered in the wrong direction and Golden Boy found her.'

'Don't tell me. The usual?'

'She accused him of rape.'

94

'Good for her.'

'He ignored her letter when she became pregnant so she wrote to his mother threatening to go to the police.'

'About time somebody did.'

'Her grace invited her here obviously to pay her off.'

'What with? They haven't got ha'pence to jingle on a tombstone. She could have given her a candlestick, of course,' laughed Ivy.

'Anyway,' concluded Fletcher, 'the girl came here and was never seen again.'

'I must say that's a new one against Golden Boy. Rape.'

'Of course, the girl could have been trying to blackmail the family.'

'Some hope.'

As Inspector Rankin drove away from the Abbey he couldn't help thinking that he should have spent more time with Ivy Jason. The presence of the ubiquitous Fletcher somehow put them both off. He was the boss of the household, of course, and the others were in awe of him. There was no doubt, however, that there was not a lot of loyalty among the staff for the Rockerby family. It was just a job as far as they were concerned in spite of having to wear what they called a stupid uniform. Famous ceilings. Famous cobwebs.

Rankin decided to visit Lazenby's in London. Ivy Jason had mentioned the name. He might be able to find out something about the missing candlestick.

He found the shop which was double-fronted with a glass door in the centre and from the windows it could be seen that the place was crammed with silver, brasses, ornamental mirrors and chandeliers of every description. There were jugs, mugs, beakers, bowls, teapots, trays, candlesticks and candelabra. Rankin looked in the windows and was amazed at what he could only call the clutter, expensive no doubt. He opened the door and walked in. A tinkling bell announced his arrival. As he stood inside the shop a small, round, bald-headed man came to meet him.

'Good morning,' he said.

'Could I speak to Mr Lazenby?' asked Rankin.

'Who wants to speak to him?'

Rankin produced his identity card.

'That's odd,' said the man. 'We've never had the police here before. I'm Lazenby.'

'I only want to ask a few questions.'

'All my stock is bought from the people who own it.'

'That's what I want to ask you.'

'Go ahead.'

'Have you had any dealings with the Rockerby family?'

'Good Heavens, yes. Over the years, of course.'

'Have you had any recently?'

'No. The last time must have been nearly a year ago.'

'Can you remember what the item was?'

'Yes. It was an ornamental mirror. Huge. Beautiful.'

'You haven't received a candlestick recently?'

'No.'

'I see.'

'May I ask the reason for these questions?'

'A candlestick has gone missing at the Abbey.'

'And they sent for you?'

'Oh, no. It's part of another enquiry.'

'Well, I'm afraid I can't help you, Inspector.'

'Thank you for your time, Mr Lazenby.'

As Rankin walked away from the shop he thought of the remark made by Ivy Jason that the duchess had sent a candlestick to be valued. It hadn't arrived yet at Lazenby's. It was obviously intended to be sold, not valued. Ivy Jason was aware of the family's little tricks and was not averse to passing them on.

Back at his quarters, Rankin was asked by his superintendent what progress he was making with the Janet Harvey case.

'Not a lot,' admitted Rankin.

'Did you get anywhere with the Abbey crowd?'

'Not really. But I'm still convinced the answer is there.'

'She was already dead when she was dumped here and you think the answer is there, not here?'

'Yes. She had a return ticket so she had no need of a lift from anybody, safari or fairground. Unless she was attracted to someone.'

'That's possible. A normal pick-up with the usual tragic result. Sex, in other words.'

'No.'

'Why not?'

'It doesn't go with the family. The family atmosphere that I've seen at the house.'

'Daughters don't always take after parents. This Janet person could have been a bit of a rebel. It happens in families.'

'No.'

'You're not convinced?'

'No.'

'You're not intimidated by the Abbey aristocracy, are you?'

'No. Not particularly. But I have to be sure of myself before confronting them.'

'You've told them that the girl was moved after being killed.'

'Oh, yes.'

'The girl accused Lord Newton of rape and threatened to contact the police. After that he must have been at his wit's end.'

'I don't think Lord Newton killed her.'

'Why not?'

'When the girl was being interviewed by the duchess he was in the safari park.'

'Can you believe that?'

'The butler told me.'

'What about the sister? Where was she?'

'She was in the building but I'm told she was busy on St John's Ambulance business.'

'Have you checked?'

'With the butler, yes.'

'I think you should talk to the duchess.'

'I will.'

When he left the superintendent's office Rankin rang the Abbey, knowing from experience that Fletcher, the butler, would answer the phone.

'Mr Fletcher?' said Rankin.

'Speaking.'

'Inspector Rankin.'

'Oh. Hello.'

'I'm afraid I need to trouble you again.'

'No trouble, Inspector. How can I help?'

'I would like to make an appointment with the duchess.'

'If you'll hold the line I'll go and ask her.'

'Thank you.'

Rankin waited for some time and even wondered

if he should telephone again but he eventually heard Fletcher's voice on the phone.

'Are you there?'

'Yes.'

'Her grace will see you at four o'clock tomorrow.'

'Thank you. I'll be there.'

'See you then.'

As he anticipated, the duchess was not alone when he called. Both Lord Newton and Lady Pamela were with her and there had evidently been some kind of conference between them.

'This is becoming rather tedious, Inspector,' said the duchess, imperiously.

'I'm sorry, your grace,' admitted Rankin, 'but there are some questions I must ask.'

'Why us?'

'Because you are the only people who can tell me what I want to know. After all, a girl is dead.'

'I'm sorry about that,' conceded the duchess, 'but I still fail to see what it has to do with us.'

'She was last seen here.'

'So you say.'

'When you interviewed the girl here, your grace, was there anyone with you?'

'No. Just the two of us.'

'You and . . .'

'The girl. Whatever her name was.'

Lord Newton and Lady Pamela sat mutely watching their mother. Rankin had a feeling that they were anxious about what she might say.

'Did the girl threaten you in any way?' asked Rankin.

'Not physically.'

'In what way?'

'She made certain accusations against my son.'

'As she said in her letter.'

'Yes.'

'They were accusations, not threats.'

'She threatened to go to the police.'

'On what charge?'

'Why, this rape business.'

'Huh!' scoffed Lord Newton.

'Did the interview take place only in this room?'

'Yes.'

Rankin looked about the room.

'I understand that a candlestick is missing from here,' he said.

'Really?' queried the duchess. 'Who told you that?'

'I'm not at liberty to disclose my source of information,' declared Rankin.

'Staff tittle-tattle,' Lord Newton scoffed again.

'It's true,' admitted the duchess. 'A candlestick is missing. I sent it up to Lazenby's to be valued.'

'I've been to Lazenby's. He says he hasn't had anything from you in nearly a year.'

'He wouldn't have got it yet. I sent it by post and you know how long that takes.'

'I see.'

'What else do you want to know?' asked the duchess.

'I would like to ask Lord Newton a question.'

'Oh,' said Freddy. 'Now me.'

'You and your sister went to a midnight party recently,' said Rankin.

'Did we?' queried Freddy. 'Yes. That's right.'

'God!' exclaimed Pamela. 'What a night that was. We didn't get home till breakfast time. The only person up was Fletcher who opened the door for us.'

'Where was the party?' asked Rankin.

'In London,' said Freddy. 'At the Continental Hotel.'

'Was it a special function? A charity event?'

'No. Purely personal. A last-minute decision.'

'We should have stayed the night instead of driving back,' asserted Pamela.

'You drove yourself?'

'Of course.'

'Which car did you use?'

'My own.'

'And which is that?'

'Range Rover.'

'Where is it now?'

'In the garage.'

'Do you mind if I have a look at it?'

'Not at all. Fletcher will show you where it is.'

'In that case,' concluded Rankin, 'I will leave you with many thanks for putting up with my questions.'

Rankin made his silent way out of the room. The other three neither said anything nor did anything. They just watched him go. Once he was outside the duchess ran to the door to make sure that he had gone. She turned to the other two.

'How did he find out about Lazenby?' she asked.

'He's been talking to the staff,' said Pamela.

'Which ones? I'll fire 'em.'

'That's one thing you can't take for granted, Ma, and that's loyalty. You don't suppose those people downstairs are our friends, do you?'

'I pay them,' insisted the duchess.

'Forget it, Ma. If you didn't pay them they'd leave. As simple as that.'

'You did throw the candlestick well out in the lake, didn't you, Freddy?' asked Pamela.

'Way out,' said Freddy. 'Nobody'll find that.'

'There's no mud on the car. He'll find nothing there.'

101

'I don't like it,' mused the duchess.

'Don't worry, Ma,' soothed Freddy. 'We're in the clear. Open a bottle.'

While the three aristocrats were celebrating, Rankin discovered a car rug in the back of the Range Rover. He was watched by the chauffeur, a dark, handsome young man.

'Ah!' exclaimed Rankin.

He took the rug carefully from the car.

'Have you got a polythene bag or something I can put this in?' he asked.

'What do you want it for?' countered the chauffeur.

'Let Forensics have a look at it.'

'I don't know about that. I'll have to ask his lordship.'

'Then will you please do so. I'll wait.'

'You mean now?'

'Of course now. I want to take it away.'

'Hang on.'

The young chauffeur hurried away to the main building. Rankin stood waiting for some time. When the chauffeur returned he said, 'He's coming down.'

'Thank you.'

Lord Newton came striding aggressively into the courtyard where Rankin was standing by the Range Rover holding the car rug.

'What's all this about?' he demanded.

'I would like to take this car rug to Forensics,' explained Rankin. 'I'll bring it back.'

'Forensics? What's that got to do with my car rug?'

'They'll check it for hairs.'

'They'll do nothing of the sort.'

'I can get a court order if you prefer.'

'Good Heavens, man! What are you saying?'

'In the interests of...' began Rankin.

'I don't care,' interrupted Lord Newton. 'You're not taking it.'

'That, of course,' went on Rankin, 'is tantamount to perverting the course of justice, which is a criminal offence and carries...'

'But why?' insisted Lord Newton. 'Why my rug?'

'Because, as I explained, the girl in question was last seen here and did not return and there is evidence that she was wrapped in a car rug.'

'Are you suggesting that she was in that rug? My rug?'

'By the process of elimination...'

'Balls! Do you think I wrapped her up and dumped her? Do you even think I killed her?'

'For the purpose of elimination I would seize on any rug I found in this area and I must warn you again that perverting the course of justice is a criminal offence.'

'I know all that. But what you're doing at the moment is accusing me of killing the girl.'

'Not you personally.'

'Someone on the estate.'

'That's a possibility.'

'You've got a bloody nerve.'

'I'm only doing my duty, my lord. After all a girl is dead and her parents are grieving. That is sometimes forgotten.'

'To hell with you,' exploded Lord Newton. 'Take the bloody rug.'

He turned on his heel and strode away.

'Have you got a bag?' Rankin asked the chauffeur.

'Somewhere,' answered the chauffeur. 'I'll have a look.'

'Thank you.'

When the chauffeur returned with a bag he asked, 'What's all this about, then?'

103

'You heard,' said Rankin.

'I've only heard that some girl came here complaining about Golden Boy.'

'And hasn't been seen since. Or, rather, she has been seen but murdered.'

'Not here?'

'She was found near her home.'

'Then why the rug?'

'She wasn't killed at her home. She was dumped there from somewhere else.'

'Oh. I see.'

Once Rankin had the car rug safely wrapped up in a polythene bag he tucked it under his arm and made his way to his own car on the other side of the courtyard.

The chauffeur watched him drive away and then could not wait to run indoors and tell the rest of the staff what had happened.

Lord Newton was worried himself and went to his sister.

'Don't tell Ma,' he said, 'but that bloody detective has taken our car rug away.'

'Whatever for?' asked Pamela.

'Forensics. They think they might find the girl's hair on it.'

'Some hope,' said Pamela. 'I got Bennett to wash it next day.'

'You did?' said Freddy, delighted.

'I thought it had got a bit smelly.'

'Bless you, darling,' enthused Freddy. 'I tried to stop him taking it which only made him more suspicious.'

'I didn't think to tell you.'

'He'll have a shock,' laughed Freddy. 'He was so cock-a-hoop.'

'He's a persistent bastard.'

Rankin's hopes were indeed dashed when Forensics told him that the car rug had been recently cleaned. It increased his suspicions, however. Why was it cleaned? And so recently.

His next effort to unravel the mystery of the murder of Janet Harvey was to make another visit to Mr Lazenby. He considered that sufficient time had elapsed for a parcel, even by slow post, to have arrived from the Abbey. Again it was a false alarm. No parcel had arrived and, apart from Mr Lazenby promising to let him know when it did arrive, Rankin's frustration was complete.

As his superintendent pointed out, 'Car rug blank. Lazenby blank. Candlestick blank.'

'I'm not so sure about that,' suggested Rankin.

'What? The candlestick?'

'Yes.'

'Don't tell me you want a search warrant. It'll take ages to search that vast Abbey drawer by drawer and cupboard by cupboard. No matter how many men you put on it, which we can't afford in any case.'

'I was thinking of the lake.'

'Ah?'

'I'd like it dredged.'

'Dredged? The cost of that plus repairing the damage would be enormous. Wouldn't frogmen do?'

'Yes. They'll do.'

'Good. I'll organise it. You inform the Abbey.'

'Right.'

Rankin did not think it necessary to visit the Abbey to advise the family of his intention so he rang Fletcher, who had almost become his friend.

'Fletcher,' he said on the phone, 'we've decided to investigate the lake at the Abbey.'

'What does that mean?' asked Fletcher. 'What happens?'

'We'll be bringing police frogmen in to search the bottom of the lake. Will you advise her grace?'

'Don't you want to wait while I tell her?'

'I'd better.'

'Be as quick as I can.'

Rankin sat in his office holding the line while Fletcher contacted the duchess. He had to wait a long time which suggested to him that the duchess was making difficulties. He was not mistaken.

'Are you there?' asked Fletcher.

'Yes, Fletcher. I'm still here.'

'The duchess objects to your proposal and will only submit if she has written authority from the chief constable.'

'I see.'

'Sorry about that, Inspector. The duchess is adamant and furious.'

'As I expected.'

'What will you do?'

'She will have her authority.'

'Good luck.'

'Thanks.'

All that Rankin could do in the face of such opposition was return to his superintendent and plead for the necessary written authority.

'The duchess is determined not to help, isn't she?' commented the superintendent.

'I'm afraid so.'

'She almost qualifies for perverting.'

'She puts a lot of faith in the chief constable who, she says, is her great friend.'

'Don't worry, Rankin. I'll put him in the picture.'

'Thank you, sir.'

When the duchess received her letter from her so-called friend, the chief constable, she started throwing her weight about. She screamed for her son who came running to her room.

'Read that!' she demanded, handing him the letter.

Freddy read the chief constable's letter and, handing back the letter said, 'You can't go against that.'

'Who can't? I'll get him on the phone straight away.'

She went to the telephone and dialled the number which she read from the letter. She waited. Then she said, 'I would like to speak to Sir Charles Evans.'

'Who wants to speak to him?'

'The Duchess of Rockerby.'

'Will you hold the line?'

The duchess waited.

'You're wasting your time,' put in Freddy.

The duchess held up her hand for silence.

'Charles?' she said.

'What can I do for you, Daphne?' asked the chief constable.

'I've got this missive from you authorising the police to dredge my lake.'

'Not dredge. They only want a couple of frogmen to do some searching.'

'Well, I don't like it. I don't want it. Can't you stop it?'

'It's police business, Daphne. I can't interfere with that.'

'But you're the chief constable, damn it.'

'The Brampton police have put me in the picture.'

'They're accusing me?'

'No, they're not. It's called the process of elimination. Finding the people who are not involved.'

'What happens if I bar them from coming here?'

'You lay yourself open to a charge of perverting the course of justice, which is a finable offence.'

'So you can't help me?'

'Not in this. Sorry.'

'Fat lot of use,' mumbled the duchess as she put the phone down.

She turned to Freddy in defiance.

'Don't let them in,' she cried.

'You can't stop them, Ma,' said Freddy who, with his sister, had listened to the duchess talking to the chief constable.

'Oh, yes, I can. This is my property. I'll have all the security people we can get patrolling the place to keep them out. I'll get Fletcher to organise it.'

'You'll be arrested for obstruction, Mother,' Pamela pointed out.

'Can you imagine the mess they'll make?'

'They'll clean it all up,' said Freddy. 'They're duty bound to do so.'

'If you try to stop them, Mother, it will only make them more suspicious.'

'Like the business with the car rug,' said Freddy. 'I had to give in.'

'All right,' said the duchess. 'I'll take your advice.'

Then, as a sudden thought, she asked, 'Do you remember where you threw the candlestick, Freddy?'

'Vaguely,' replied Freddy.

'Couldn't you get it back before the police arrive?'

'I haven't got a wetsuit.'

'You can get one.'

'It'll need more than that, Mother,' put in Pamela.

108

'You need a mask, breathing apparatus. I couldn't do it.'

'Freddy could, couldn't you, Freddy?'

'Ma!' complained Freddy. 'It means crawling about on the bottom of the lake. I'm no diver. Besides, what are the staff going to think if they see me doing that?'

'You're not helping me. Either of you,' complained the duchess.

'I'll get a rake and see if I can find it near the edge,' offered Freddy.

'You said you threw it right out in the middle,' the duchess reminded him.

'It may have moved.'

'How could it? It's not tidal. All it has to move it is the fountain.'

'They may not find it anyway.'

'Don't be daft, Freddy,' said the duchess. 'A brass candlestick will stand out a mile. It'll be shiny.'

'No,' said Freddy. 'It's in a black plastic bag.'

'Oh, good.'

'Well done, Freddy,' said Pamela.

'I couldn't very well walk about the grounds with a bloody great candlestick in my hand. If anyone had seen they'd think it odd to say the least. But wrapped up in a parcel, well that's ordinary untidiness.'

The duchess sat in her armchair, musing.

'If only I hadn't killed the bloody girl.'

'If only Freddy hadn't raped her,' said Pamela.

'If only she hadn't been in that room,' concluded Freddy.

The Abbey staff were all agog when they saw the police frogmen arrive and Fletcher spent his time trying to answer questions that the rest of the staff kept asking him. He could not answer them because he did not know. All the staff were aware of was that the one they called Golden Boy had caused some kind of trouble, which was nothing new to them, but this new turn of events was exciting.

'What are they looking for?' said Ivy. 'They found her. It said so in the papers.'

The two of them were watching the proceedings about the lake from an upstairs window.

'You know the inspector,' urged Ivy. 'Why don't you ask him?'

'I can't interfere,' protested Fletcher.

The duchess and her son and daughter watched the frogmen's efforts from their apartment.

It was a large lake and the frogmen made several attempts to locate the candlestick that Inspector Rankin suspected could be at the bottom. Each time the frogmen came up with nothing Rankin, standing by, would urge them to more effort. The frogmen were becoming exasperated and angry at what appeared to be a futile operation consisting of their crawling along the bottom of what could only be silt and soil.

And then, suddenly, one of the men broke the surface of the water like a Jack-in-the-box and held up something wrapped in polythene. He scrambled out of the water and handed the prize to Rankin. Rankin thanked the frogman and took the object to his car. He opened the boot, laid the object in it and began to remove the polythene. A large, heavy, golden candlestick was revealed.

'Just as I thought,' he muttered.

'OK?' asked the frogman.

'Fine. Thank you for finding it.'

'It wasn't easy.'

'I can see it wasn't. I can now take it to Forensics and see what they make of it.'

'They've found something!' cried Ivy Jason as she stood at the window with Fletcher.

'Something wrapped up by the look of it,' said Fletcher.

'What are they going to do with it?'

'Take it to Forensics. That's what they usually do. You've seen it on television.'

'What for?'

'Fingerprints and that sort of thing. I don't know.'

'Fingerprints in the water?' queried Ivy.

'I said I don't know. Come on. It's all over. Back to work.'

As Fletcher made his way downstairs from the landing that had been his viewpoint there was a knock at the front door. He opened it to reveal Inspector Rankin without the parcel.

'Will you thank her grace for allowing us to search the lake?' said Rankin.

'I certainly will, Inspector.' Then he couldn't help asking, 'Did you find what you were looking for?'

'That remains to be seen.'

'Nothing I can tell her grace?'

'Not at this stage.'

'Fair enough.'

'Cheers.'

'Cheers.'

Rankin walked away to his car and drove back to Brampton anxious to deliver the candlestick to Forensics.

When Freddy, who was watching the lake with the duchess and his sister, saw the frogman wave something in the air he recognised the parcel that he had thrown into the lake.

'That's done it!' exclaimed Pamela. 'They've found it.'

'Do you think it's the candlestick?' asked the duchess.

'It can't be anything else,' said Pamela.

'What do we do now?' asked the duchess.

'I know,' said Freddy, eagerly, 'if the inspector comes sniffing around we say an intruder must have made off with it and in his panic threw it in the lake.'

'That's an idea,' said the duchess.

'Clever Freddy,' added Pamela.

Little did the family realise just what evidence the candlestick was to reveal. Inspector Rankin read the report submitted to him by the forensic branch. Apart from fingerprints, a certain number of hairs were stuck to the blood on it and these corresponded with the hair of Janet Harvey. There could be nothing more straightforward than that, thought Rankin. It only remained now to verify whose fingerprints were on the candlestick. This would involve taking someone with him to the Abbey with a portable apparatus.

He telephoned the Abbey.

'Mr Fletcher?'

'Speaking.'

'Inspector Rankin.'

'Why, hello.'

'I need to see the duchess and her son and daughter,' said Rankin. 'Can you arrange a time for me?'

'I will go to her grace immediately if you will hold on.'

'Thank you.'

Rankin waited. He did not intend to reveal to the Abbey the fact that he would be taking their fingerprints. He anticipated a certain amount of rebellion anyway, without such added aggravation as a fingerprint machine. While he was ruminating Fletcher returned to the phone.

'Are you there?'

'Hello. Yes.'

'Her grace will see you on Thursday at four o'clock.'

'I also need to see Lord Newton and Lady Pamela.'

'I have made that clear.'

'Oh good. Thank you.'

Although the date was a week ahead, he was quite sure that very little could change in the meantime unless the three culprits, as he considered them, decided to run away. Which was most unlikely. It would not be difficult to pick them up anyway, so he wasn't worried.

Fletcher was surprised when Inspector Rankin presented himself at the Abbey accompanied by a colleague.

'Oh,' said Fletcher. 'Two of you?'

'Yes,' explained Rankin. 'This is Detective Clarke.'

'How do you do?' said Fletcher.

Detective Clarke merely nodded.

The duchess was more than surprised. She was indignant. She was horrified to see Inspector Rankin's assistant carrying some kind of metal attaché case.

'I thought we were receiving only you, Inspector,' remarked the duchess, haughtily.

'This is my assistant, Detective Clarke,' said Rankin. 'He is here to conduct the fingerprinting.'

'Fingerprinting?' echoed the duchess. 'What are we? Criminals?'

'With your permission, your grace...' began Rankin.

'Which I certainly withhold,' interrupted the duchess.

113

'In that case I must summon all three of you to appear at your local police station to comply with the tests.'

'But this is outrageous!' cried the duchess.

'Doing it this way would avoid newspaper publicity. That was my reason. As you probably know, reporters automatically call at local police stations in search of a story and I'm sure they'd be delighted to learn that such local luminaries as yourselves were being fingerprinted following the murder of a girl named Janet Harvey.'

A silence followed.

Lord Newton stepped up to the Inspector.

'You can take my prints, Inspector,' he said.

'Thank you, my lord.'

Detective Clarke assembled his apparatus and Lady Pamela and the duchess watched as Freddy moved his fingers over the absorbent pad. The detective gave him a cloth to wipe his fingers afterwards.

'Nothing to it,' he declared. 'Have a go, Pam.'

Lady Pamela submitted to the fingerprinting.

'Would someone explain to me the purpose of his charade?' asked the duchess.

'The purpose, your grace,' explained Rankin, 'is to establish who handled the candlestick that was recovered from the lake here.'

'That all?' she remarked.

'Have a go, Ma,' urged Freddy. 'Your prints will go down for posterity.'

The duchess shook her head.

'You know what I think, Inspector?' suggested Freddy. 'I think some intruder ran off with it, panicked and threw it in the lake.'

'Sounds reasonable,' added Lady Pamela.

'That's quite possible, of course,' agreed Rankin,

'in normal circumstances, but in this case there were human hairs stuck to the candlestick that corresponded to the hairs on the head of Janet Harvey.'

'What!' exclaimed Freddy.

'I'm afraid so,' confirmed Rankin. 'Forensics are quite definite.'

'You mean she was murdered?' asked Freddy.

'Oh, yes,' replied Rankin. 'I thought you understood that. It was in the papers.'

'Then we're suspects,' he cried, 'with all this fingerprinting business.'

'Not suspects,' explained Rankin. 'It's what we call the process of elimination.'

'Good God. Did you realise that, Pam?'

'Well, I never thought the inspector was inviting us to a garden party,' said Lady Pamela.

'Would you oblige, please, your grace?' asked Rankin.

'Oh, all right,' said the grand lady. 'If I don't you'll only suspect us more.'

As the duchess submitted to the fingerprinting process she declared, 'You'll find plenty of my prints on that candlestick plus half the staff. They've nearly all handled it at some time or other.'

Inspector Rankin made no comment and when the process was concluded Freddy cried, 'Well done, Ma.'

'What happens now?' asked the duchess.

'We leave you in peace,' said Rankin.

'Thank God for that,' she muttered.

'We hand everything over to Forensics,' said Rankin.

'Forensics,' scoffed Freddy. 'I don't know what you lot would do without Forensics.'

'Neither do I,' confessed Rankin, as he went out of the room with Detective Clarke.

He returned to his own police station where he had another meeting with the superintendent.

'Do you plan to arrest the duchess?' asked the superintendent.

'She's obviously guilty,' admitted Rankin.

'Then have her in. Get her to make a statement and we'll take it from there. I expect she'll be bailed so she can go home until her case comes up.'

'She'll make trouble,' laughed Rankin.

'Take a marked car and Clarke. She won't get any change out of the chief constable if she tries that one.'

'A marked car outside the Abbey,' mused Rankin. 'That'll cause a stir.'

Which it did. The staff were all gazing out of the windows as Rankin pulled up at the front door in the colourful police car driven by Detective Clarke.

Fletcher opened the door for the two men before they had a chance to ring or knock.

'I would like to see her grace,' said Rankin.

'I'll tell her.'

Fletcher climbed the stairs and came back to escort the two policemen to the apartment where the duchess was in the company of her son and daughter.

'You again?' said the duchess.

'Your grace,' declared Rankin. 'I have here a warrant for your arrest and I...'

Before Rankin could finish his sentence the duchess let out a scream and fell back into an armchair.

'I don't believe it,' she gasped.

'Now look here, Inspector,' began Freddy, aggressively.

Rankin held up his hand so that he could conclude his remarks.

'I have a warrant for your arrest for the murder of Janet Harvey. You don't have to say anything but...'

'Oh, blah, blah. The usual,' said Freddy. 'We've seen it all on television.'

There was a sudden silence. Pamela went to her mother and put an arm round her.

'Don't worry, Ma. It must be some mistake,' she said.

'There's no mistake,' asserted Rankin. 'I would like you to come with me to Brampton police station to make a statement, your grace. Then you can come back here and wait until the trial, whenever that might be.'

'You're not locking her up?' asked Pamela.

'No,' said Rankin. 'We just want a statement. In her own words.'

'Why can't she make it at the local here?' asked Freddy.

'The body was discovered at Brampton and the Brampton police have charge of the case.'

'Are you taking here in the police car?' asked Pamela.

'I'm afraid so,' admitted Rankin.

'It'll be handcuffs next,' scoffed the duchess.

'No, it won't,' Pamela assured her.

'You can follow in your car, if you wish, my lord,' suggested Rankin. 'Then you can take her grace back when she's made her statement.'

'We'll do that,' said Freddy. 'Won't we, Pam?'

'Of course.'

Then Freddy suddenly remembered something and nearly fell into a trap.

'Wait a minute,' he said. 'We don't know the way.'

He and Pamela exchanged significant glances.

'No bother,' said Rankin, producing a piece of paper from his pocket. 'Here's the map I've been using on my way to and from here.'

'Oh, thanks,' said Freddy, examining the paper.

'Your grace?' prompted Rankin.

The duchess heaved herself out of her chair.

'I'd better take a coat, Pamela,' she said.

'I'll get one.'

Lady Pamela hurried out of the room.

'I'll meet you downstairs,' she said.

Rankin led the way, followed by the duchess who was followed by Detective Clarke.

'I'll get the car and follow you,' said Freddy, hurrying on ahead.

The staff of the Abbey watched from windows as the duchess was helped into the police car. Ivy Jason was standing next to Fletcher.

'What do you make of that?' she asked.

'Very sad,' said Fletcher.

'Are they going to lock her up?'

'Of course not.'

'Pity. What are they taking her away for then?'

'Questioning I expect.'

'About that girl?'

'Oh, yes.'

'I was hoping they'd keep her for a bit.'

'Not before the trial.'

'Trial? Christ! Bad as that, is it?'

''Fraid so.'

'Shit!'

'Come on now. Back to work.'

'Perhaps we won't see her again after that,' concluded Ivy. 'That would be good, wouldn't it?'

No sooner had the duchess arrived at Brampton police station that one or two locals 'in the know' heard about it, though the press were not informed.

One of those 'in the know' was Janet's father, a town hall official, who could not wait to tell his wife.

'They've got the duchess,' he declared.

'Who has? What are you talking about?' asked Mother, irritably.

'They've got the duchess at the police station on a charge of Janet's murder.'

'No!'

'I got it from the sergeant. It's all hush-hush at the moment.'

'It would be. Because of her.'

'I hope she gets life.'

'I wish she could swing.'

'We'll get our revenge yet.'

Mother and Father held hands and hugged each other as they stood in the kitchen.

Lord Newton and Lady Pamela were sitting on a bench in Brampton police station waiting to take the duchess back to the Abbey. They had been waiting a long time.

'They're not keeping her, are they?' asked Pamela, anxiously.

'No,' said Freddy. 'They said we could take her home. They're just long-winded, that's all. And I daresay Ma's making the most of her statement.'

'I won't feel safe until we've got her indoors.'

'Neither will I.'

Their patience was eventually rewarded when they saw the duchess bearing down on them from an interrogation room down the corridor. Pamela gave her a warm hug.

'All right, Ma?' asked Freddy.

'Home, James,' said the duchess, brightly.

All three hurried out of the building to the Range Rover that was waiting outside.

119

Rankin had a final meeting with his superintendent.

'Pretty lengthy statement,' commented the superintendent.

'Typical of the lady,' said Rankin.

'She admits hitting the girl but calls it provocation.'

'Provocation with the girl's back turned?'

'Exactly,' chuckled the superintendent.

'They always wriggle.'

'Anyway, you've nailed her. Well done.'

'Thank you.'

At dinner at the Abbey that night there was a special guest, a friend of the family who happened to be the most famous barrister in the legal profession. Whether counsel for the defence or the prosecution he always seemed to win his cases. His name was Sir Charles Curran. He was a large, overweight man in his sixties, the scourge of the law courts.

He had read the letters and listened to the evidence presented to him by Freddy and his mother which took place during the dinner. At the end of it all there was an ominous silence.

Unable to bear the suspense Freddy said, 'Well?'

Charles Curran laughed. It was a very loud laugh.

'It's what is called an open and shut case, Freddy,' the great man declared. 'I've never come across one more open or more shut.'

Again he laughed, this time at his own joke.

'The young lady made one vital mistake,' explained Sir Charles. 'Money. If she hadn't mentioned money then she might have had a case.'

'As simple as that?' asked Freddy.

'As simple as that,' repeated Sir Charles.

Then he went on, 'You and your sister, of course,

are accessories after the fact for driving the girl to wherever it was but that's a mere bagatelle.'

'Thank God for that,' said Pamela.

'As it is,' continued Sir Charles, 'as an unmarried mother the girl would have had the benefit of the welfare state so her insistence on some monetary contribution from you could be a form of blackmail and, coupled with the threat of police exposure, there is a good case for the defence in provocation. Obviously no one intended to kill the girl. She brought it on herself by her intransigence and her threats. I would say you have nothing to worry about except the resultant publicity.'

'Oh, that!' muttered Pamela, dismissively.

'There you are, Ma,' said Freddy. 'I said you were in the clear.'

'Thank you, Charles,' said the duchess in a very quiet voice.

And so it transpired. All that Sir Charles Curran had predicted came true. There was a good deal of publicity during the trial, which lasted six weeks, with the duchess staying with a friend in London during that period. She was acquitted, of course, again as Sir Charles predicted, and the family at the Abbey were happy and relieved.

The parents of the murdered girl, Janet Harvey, were not so happy. They had attended the court throughout the proceedings and their hopes were raised and lowered as the lawyers argued their cases. As they left the building they were approached by a television interviewer.

'What do you think of the verdict, Mr Harvey?' he asked.

Father stood in front of the man and said, 'All I can say is there's one law for the rich and one for the poor and this verdict proves it.'

With that he pushed his way past the man and, holding his wife's hand, made his way home.

'Poor Janet,' sobbed Mother, as they walked along. 'She doesn't deserve that.'

'She certainly doesn't,' agreed Father.

'She's still dead and that woman...'

THE PICK-UP

It was a pick-up, no matter how much the two of them denied it. They had met in a bar and had 'got talking'. They were sitting on separate bar stools and she had dropped her cigarette lighter. He picked it up and handed it to her.

'Thanks.'

'Another nail in your coffin.'

'I know. I give it up occasionally.'

There was a silence after that until she asked, 'Does it bother you?'

'What?'

'The smoke.'

'No,' he said, without conviction.

'I think it does. You just don't like to say.'

She stubbed out the cigarette in the ashtray on the counter.

'You needn't have wasted it.'

'Good for me.'

'Perhaps I can buy you a drink as compensation.'

'That's very kind of you. Could I have a scotch?'

'Of course.'

He turned to the barman.

'Tony. A scotch for the lady, please.'

'You've been here before?'

'Oh, yes. Often. I'm a regular.'

'I haven't seen you here before.'

'Perhaps I was away.'

'I always come here when I can.'

The man pointed to the sign over the counter.

'Why is it always called an American Bar?'

'I've no idea.'

'Why not just bar?'

'I agree.'

'Did the Americans invent the cocktail? I suppose that's it.'

'Could be.'

They were in the bar of one of the best hotels in London.

'I'm Helen Forrest, by the way.'

'I'm Lance Harvey.'

'Lance. That's an unusual name.'

'I've had it a long time.'

'Not that long, I'd say. Middle thirties?'

'Near enough.'

'Do you live in London?'

'No. About an hour outside. In Bucks.'

'Oh, yes. Bucks and Berks.'

'You?'

'I live here. I'm an actress. Resting at the moment.'

'Should I have seen you?'

'I doubt it. No stars or leads. Only support. But it's been regular up to now.'

'Does it worry you?'

'No. Something will turn up. I'm sure my agent wants to eat as much as I do.'

'It sounds precarious.'

'I suppose it is.'

Lance studied the girl who was sitting beside him. She was certainly attractive. Her hair was black and straight with a fringe which set off her face perfectly. She was someone you would look at a second time. Her figure, as far as he could tell sitting on a stool as she was, was appealing, her legs slim and long, her breasts slightly dominant, her lips welcoming. He liked her and found her company relaxing. In his position as senior partner in a well-established architectural company, he was in the habit of dropping into the bar for a glass of champagne at the end of the day. That is, at about five o'clock.

Helen, for her part, found Lance good-looking and

good company. He was well-dressed and could evidently afford to drink champagne by the glass. Something in the City, she surmised. And yet there was something more relaxing about him that did not speak of the City as she understood it. He probably had a wife. Bound to.

Lance did have a wife. Her name was Kay and they were quite happy together. There was nothing exciting about their relationship. She was a normal woman, dutiful and efficient. She had fair, wavy hair that seemed to need the hairdresser fairly regularly. At the moment she was visiting her sister in Australia so he thought there was no need to hurry home to dinner. He was left in the hands of the Italian couple at the house in Buckinghamshire. They had been with them for several years, she doing the cooking and the man doing the cleaning. While Kay had been away, Lance's dinner hour had been somewhat erratic, which the staff took in their stride and which they would have to abandon this evening because he felt like asking his new-found friend, Helen, to dinner.

'Are you hungry?' he asked.

'Oh, no. I have a little money of my own so I can afford to rest, as it's called.'

'I'm talking about now.'

'Oh.'

'I'd like to take you to dinner.'

'That's very kind of you.'

'Where would you like to go?'

'What about here?'

'If you like.'

He turned to the barman.

'Tony, would you ask the restaurant to reserve me a table for two?'

'Certainly, Mr Harvey.'

The barman went to the house phone and dialled a number.

He came back to say, 'That's all arranged, sir.'

'Thank you.'

To Helen he said, 'One for the road?'

'Hardly a road.'

'One for the carpeted corridor.'

'Do you always drink champagne?'

'When I can. I find it safer. And there's no hangover.'

After their final drink they made their way to the restaurant, an ornate, chandelier-hung room of great elegance, famous for its good food.

During the meal they exchanged life stories. Helen's was quite simple. She had been on the stage since she was a small child. She lost both her parents in a car crash and as a result she inherited some money which, in the circumstances, helps her during her rest periods. She told her story in a matter-of-fact manner and Lance had the feeling that she was a very self-possessed person well capable of looking after herself. She lacked that sense of helplessness that was part of some women's attraction. Yet he felt she could be affectionate.

Lance had little to tell her about himself. He was an architect, he was married, he had no children. He enjoyed his work and was never happier than when he was designing some huge construction somewhere. He had designed most of the new buildings in London and to a great extent he could consider himself successful. What he could not tell Helen was the fact the he enjoyed a social life among what could be called important people, ministers, peers of the realm and so on. He found his social life helpful to his business and was indebted to his wife for introducing him to many of his clients, particularly the straight-laced zions of the Social Register. She, with her own money and original social background, was well known to them. They would frown on his present behaviour.

After dinner Lance said, 'Can I drive you home?'

'That's kind of you. Where's your car?'

'Right outside.'

'You must be a regular at that rate.'

Lance saw Helen to the car, opening the door for her.

'Tell me where,' he said, as they drove off.

With instructions such as right here, left there and so on they arrived at the building in Gloucester Gardens where Helen had her flat. It was in a road parallel to Green Park.

'Would you like to come up for coffee?' she asked.

'Yes. Thank you.'

'It's on the third floor. But there's a lift.'

'Good.'

The flat consisted of a sitting room, bedroom, bathroom and kitchen and was pleasantly furnished. As an architect Lance would have said that it was occupied by a lady of taste. He approved.

'Very nice,' he said.

'Thank you.'

'Sit down while I get the coffee.'

Lance sat on the sofa and looked about the room admiringly. Helen came into the room carrying two mugs of aromatic coffee which she placed on the low, long table in front of the sofa. They sat together before drinking the coffee and Lance found himself leaning towards Helen and kissing her on the lips. She reacted with enthusiasm and before long they had undressed each other and were making passionate love on the sofa.

When it was over and they had got their breath back Lance said, 'I didn't expect that to happen.'

'Neither did I.'

They reached for their coffee, half-dressed as they were.

'It's cold,' said Helen. 'I'll make some more.'

'No, no,' pleaded Lance. 'Don't bother.'

'Why? That's not going to happen again, is it?'

'Not at the moment. I didn't want you to go to any trouble.'

Helen took the two mugs back to the kitchen and quickly returned with freshly made coffee which she placed once more on the low table.

'This time I suggest we drink it,' she said.

'We will.'

They drank their coffee. Helen began to dress.

'Why are you dressing? You're going to bed, aren't you?'

'Habit.'

'You mean you make a habit of this?'

'God, no. Far from it. It's a habit to put your clothes on before you take them off to put them away.'

'I suppose another woman could work that out.'

'I don't want to sit here naked.'

'I see.'

'Isn't it time you dressed? Unless you're planning to stay the night.'

'Could I?'

'You'd have to sleep on the sofa.'

'No. I'll go home.'

'It's late.'

'No matter.'

'Don't fall asleep at the wheel.'

'I must see you again.'

'I'm here.'

'Same place, same stool?'

'If you like.'

'Six o'clock.'

'Six o'clock.'

Following a farewell embrace, Lance drove home. It was early morning but he was not tired. He kept thinking of what had just happened, not the sexual intercourse but the meeting. He had never experienced it before. How did it happen? He had to see the girl again. There was something about her, he didn't know what it was. Whatever it was it suited him and made him happy. Did his wife make him happy? Of course she did, but it wasn't the same. He was happily married. It wasn't just sex. That wasn't difficult to come by, if necessary. Was it mere newness, a new face, a different touch to the flesh? He didn't think so. Helen wasn't a beauty. She was attractive with a special personality. His own wife was insipid by comparison. Was that something to do with acting, stage performance? Helen wasn't 'on stage' all the time. She wasn't on stage when she was sitting on the bar stool next to him. She wasn't on stage during dinner or in the flat. He felt wanted with her, that's what it was. As for sex, he knew now that he could help himself, which gave him a pleasant feeling. He did not have that feeling with his wife. He could not imagine sitting on the sofa with his wife drinking coffee and suddenly making love. She would think he was either drunk or mad. It wouldn't even have happened when they were 'courting'. It was a question of personalities.

The staff were asleep when he arrived home. The intruder lights came on automatically as he approached the house from the long driveway. Lights had been left on in the house so that he could find his way. He turned them out as he progressed towards his bedroom. Tired as he was he could not sleep. It wasn't anxiety that kept him awake it was more an insistent thinking. He could not stop thinking yet he would find it difficult to explain to anyone what he was thinking about.

In the office next morning his partner made his usual entrance and his usual, 'How goes it?'

'Hello, Gordon,' said Lance.

Gordon Cooper was the only other partner in their architectural business. He was an easy-going character and Lance relied on him more for administration within the company than any inspired contribution to a project.

'Wife still away?' asked Gordon.

'Yes.'

'You look well on it. Early nights obviously suit you.'

The poor man couldn't be more wrong thought Lance but he went along with it. Little did he know. In spite of their closeness to each other in business and as school friends years before, Lance could not discuss Helen with him. They could only discuss wives, their own, Gordon being a cousin of Lance's wife. There had never been anyone else to discuss until now.

At the stroke of five o'clock Lance left the office. This was unusual. Gordon would normally go into Lance's office at five o'clock for what he called a conference but Lance was determined to get away. He brushed his partner aside.

'Save till the morning,' he called out.

Gordon stood dumfounded. Such a thing had never happened before.

Lance took his car from the car park at the rear of the building and drove to the same hotel that he had visited the evening before. The commissionaire met him and opened the door for him.

'Good evening, Mr Harvey.'

'Evening, Edward.'

'I'll put it away for you.'

'Thank you.'

Lance enjoyed a similar privilege in several hotels in London that he was in the habit of frequenting.

Helen was sitting on a stool already when he made his way to the bar.

'Beat me to it,' he said.

'Only five minutes,' she admitted.

'Evening, Tony.'

'Good evening, sir.'

'What does one say to an architect?' asked Helen. 'Had a good day at the drawing board?'

'You could say, "Any bridges fallen down lately"?'

'Oh, God. I hope not.'

'What about you?'

'I went to an audition this morning.'

'Oh.'

'I don't hold out much hope.'

'Why not?'

'Instinct.'

'Then why did you go?'

'My agent suggested it. If I didn't go he might not recommend me next time.'

'Don't you find it embarrassing?'

133

'No.'

After a couple of drinks Lance asked, 'What would you like to do this evening?'

'What about the cinema?'

'Cinema?'

'I'd like to see that thing at the Odeon.'

'Fine. We'll leave the car here and go by taxi.'

'Can you do that?'

'Oh, yes. Then we'll come back here and pick it up.'

'Privilege,' scoffed Helen.

'No. Habit.'

During the running of the film, which Lance didn't find very interesting, he put his hand on Helen's thigh. While looking at the screen with rapt attention she opened her legs so that he could feel the soft flesh above the top of her stockings. She made no attempt to touch him.

At the end of the film, as they got up to leave, Helen asked, 'Did you enjoy that?'

'Yes. But not the film.'

'I loved it.'

'Where now?'

'The flat?'

'Why not?'

Arriving back at the hotel in a taxi Lance suggested, 'One for the road?'

'Yes. I could do with one after that film.'

They made their way to the bar and after a refreshing glass of whisky for one and champagne for the other, they left in Lance's car and drove to Helen's flat.

'Good Heavens!' exclaimed Lance, suddenly.

'What?'

'I haven't given you any dinner.'

'Don't worry. I'm not hungry. Are you?'

'Not particularly. Eating's a habit, anyway.'

Once in the flat Helen pushed Lance into the sofa, dropped to her knees and unzipped his trousers.

'Darling...' he breathed.

He did not touch her in case he upset her hair-do. He simply gripped the arm of the sofa until it was all over. Then Helen climbed up and kissed him on the lips passionately. He pulled her dress up and fondled her bottom and between her legs. They slipped to the floor, still tightly embraced and made love on the carpet. When it was all over they climbed back onto the sofa to recover their breath.

'That was a bit of a scramble, wasn't it?' said Helen with a laugh.

'You're wonderful,' gasped Lance.

'It's a good job your wife's not here. She could tell.'

'Do you think so?'

'Women always can. They don't always call attention to it.'

'I hope not.'

'Have you done much of this before?'

'This? What do you mean, this?'

'Extramarital whatever it's called.'

'No.'

'No?'

'I've never bothered.'

'So why now? What's the difference?'

'You.'

'You mean I'm not the ordinary pick-up?'

'You're not a pick-up at all.'

'But that's how all this happened.'

'It was not a pick-up.'

'You don't know that I didn't set out to lure you.'

'Lure me?'

Lance laughed at the use of such a word.

'What does lure mean?' he asked. 'I associate it with mermaids on rocks luring sailors to their death.'

'Is that what they did?'

'According to legend.'

'You don't know that I didn't drop my lighter purposely.'

'As a matter of fact I thought you dropped it because you were pissed.'

Now it was Helen's turn to laugh.

'Pissed? Because I was drinking whisky, I suppose.'

'Yes. I thought you were a barfly.'

'You certainly swatted me. What made you change your mind?'

'It didn't take long to realise you were far from pissed.'

'Thank you.'

'Or I wouldn't have spoken to you. Besides, I don't think Tony Barman would have let you get that far. I've seen him refuse drinks to customers he thinks have had enough. Usually Americans who start making a nuisance of themselves. "Hey, Bud, nobody refuses me a drink." You know the scene.'

'Very well.'

'Incidentally, why do you drink whisky?'

'Doctor's orders.'

'What!'

'It's good for my heart. In moderation, of course.'

'I never knew that.'

'Oh, yes.'

'Is something wrong with your heart?'

'Not really. Some irregularity I think they call it.'

'Nothing serious?'

'No.'

'Good. I don't want to lose you when I've only just met you.'

'I wonder if you'll say that when I'm old and grey.'
'I'll be old and grey, too, so we won't notice it.'
'Is that how it goes?'
'I think so. I want to go on meeting you. I know that.'
'Do you?'
'Of course.'
'I wasn't taking it for granted.'
'Neither am I. It's just a wish.'
'And your wish will be granted, Oh Lord.'
'Thank you.'

As Lance pulled Helen close to him she cried, 'No! No! It's late and you have a long drive.'

Lance was aware of the time but tried to ignore it. It was only because he thought that Helen might be tired and want to go to bed that he eventually decided to kiss her goodnight.

'Good night, darling.'
'Good night, dear.'
'Save a stool for me if you're first.'
'I will.'

As Lance drove home he wondered what he would do about Helen when his wife, Kay, arrived back from Australia. He would still meet her at the bar and as long as he was home to dinner there would be no difference. He wouldn't be able to stay as long as this. It would have to be one of those five till seven affairs, which he did not consider satisfactory. He wanted time to linger, not just make love and vanish. Yet he could not think of any other way round it. To save time he would suggest meeting at Helen's instead of the American Bar of the hotel. It was making a convenience of her but he didn't think

137

she would mind that. She could refuse, of course, but he hoped she wouldn't. The idea of losing her frightened him.

They discussed the problem when they met the next evening. From the American Bar they progressed to the flat and after their usual tussle on the carpet they lay talking.

'This is what I'm going to miss, of course,' said Lance.

'Sex?'

'No. Talking.'

'Don't you talk after having sex with your wife?'

'If we do it's about new curtains or carpet. That is, if we have sex.'

'But you do, surely?'

'Rarely. It's what happens to married couples. It wears off. It's nice to relax with you and chat afterwards. The afterwards is the most important part of sex.'

'You mean sex or love?'

'Love? I suppose we all need two people. One here, one there. One for this, one for that.'

'I've been told there are things a man would not do to his wife but would do to another woman.'

'You mean some kind of deviation?'

'It's odd, you know. They'd do it in a field, in the back of a car so long as they weren't married. As soon as they're married things change.'

'How do you know?'

'I'm quite capable of doing my own research.'

'Clever girl.'

'For instance. Now I'll put you to the test.'

'Go on.'

'Do you do to your wife what you do to me?'

'I...'

'Come on. Honest.'

'Not quite.'

'Not quite? What on earth does that mean?'

'Well, there's a difference.'

'That's what I want to know.'

'All right. The answer's no.'

'Do you ask her to do to you what you ask me to do?'

'No.'

'Why not?'

'Because she's my wife.'

'Does that mean if we were married we'd stop doing certain things?'

'It's possible.'

'And I suppose you would then go after someone else, some other pick-up, as you have done now.'

'You're not an actress, darling. You're a bloody psychologist.'

'They go together.'

'I've never associated the acting profession with a great deal of intelligence. Until now. Particularly the men. I mean they have to rely on what someone has written before they can say anything. I don't mean to offend you.'

'I'm not offended. I agree with you as far as men are concerned. They're thick. But women? I would only agree with you when it came to pin-ups and similar birds of paradise. In any case, women are brighter than men at any time.'

'I agree. Otherwise they'd be mere manipulative tools.'

'Speaking of tools...'

They laughed as they kissed and fell to making love again. It was their last time unhindered as Lance's wife was due home.

* * *

Lance met Kay at Heathrow on her arrival from Australia. They hugged and kissed decorously with a peck on the cheek. On the way home in the car his wife chatted enthusiastically about her trip, her visit to her sister and friends, what a wonderful place Perth was with the Swan river and colourful parks.

'You should have come,' she said.

'Next time.'

'That's what you always say.'

'It's a long way. So long you have to stay long enough to make it worth while. I haven't always got the time.'

'I know. I just wished you were there. I wanted to share it with you.'

She brought presents for the Italian couple who looked after the house and a special present for Lance which was a sculptured head of a young girl produced by a famous Aborigine artist.

She was still talking about her trip at dinner and even in bed. All that Lance had to do was listen and make appropriate mutterings in response, which amused him.

They did not make love, which also amused him.

What Lance and Helen called the 'new arrangement' now took place. Gone was the bar stool meeting in the interest of what they considered cynically as Time and Motion. So Lance made his way directly to Helen's flat. He parked the car and took the lift to her floor. As he reached the landing he saw a man coming out of her door, closing the door carefully after him. The man was well-dressed, good-looking

140

in a dark, swarthy way and in his thirties. Lance stood and watched him go down in the lift. He then rang the bell on Helen's door. She opened it at once and he went in.

'Who was that?' he demanded.

'Oh, did you see him? That's Harry Ball.'

'What was he doing here?'

'He dropped in for a chat.'

'Does he often do that?'

'Every now and then.'

'Why?'

'He's an old friend.'

'What does he mean to you?'

Helen laughed.

'What is this? A catechism?'

'I didn't expect to find anyone here.'

'I do have friends, you know. You don't have to be jealous.'

'I'm not jealous.'

'Of course you are. I'm flattered.'

'I asked you what he meant to you. You haven't answered.'

'He's only a friend.'

'Where did you meet him?'

'In the theatre. He's an actor. He tipped me off about a play that's going into production.'

'He could have done that on the phone.'

'Not with the script.'

Helen went to the sideboard and showed Lance the script of the play in question.

'Was he your lover?'

'Him?'

'Yes.'

'Heavens, no. He's as gay as a peacock with his feathers out.'

'He could be ambi.'

'Now you're looking for trouble. I said you were jealous.'

'All right. I admit it. I am.'

'Why? You have a wife. I should be jealous.'

'I have a wife and you.'

'Oh, like that, is it?'

'Do you mind?'

'Not at all. It would be nice to be asked first.'

'You started it by dropping your lighter.'

'When I lured you, you mean?'

They both laughed.

'Yes,' said Lance. 'I didn't know I would enjoy being lured so much. I always considered it something sinister.'

Once they had made love and settled down Lance looked at the clock.

'I have to watch the time,' he said.

'I know. That's what's so unfair. You arrive at five and go at seven. What do I do then?'

'Whatever you did before you met me.'

'You mean back on my stool and dropping my lighter again?'

'No. Don't do that.'

'Why not?'

'I'm serious.'

'You don't own me, dear. I'm only on hire.'

'Don't talk like that. Please.'

'Why not?'

'Because I ... I almost love you.'

'Darling! That's the most honest thing I've ever heard a man say.'

'Oh, don't go all learned.'

'I almost love you, too.'

It was true. That's how they felt about each other.

When Lance was making love to her he wanted to say, 'I love you' but realised he used to say it to his wife and could not bring himself to say it again. One or other of the statements could not be true. Not entirely. Almost. He wanted to love her. He did love her but could not bring himself to say so. He was fonder of her than he was his wife. He was prepared to admit that much. Yet he wouldn't dream of leaving his wife. Apart from the social upheaval, he feared that his business would be affected. Fortunately, he thought, they had no children so there could be no complications in that respect. He was content to allow the affair to drift on as it was at the moment but he knew within himself that the routine could not last in its present form. Something had to happen. He had to see her more often and for longer periods. But how? He couldn't make out that pressure of work kept him at the office, a change that would be so sudden as to be obvious. His wife knew enough about his work habits to recognise the lie.

'Darling,' he mused, 'what are we going to do?'

'About us?'

'Yes.'

'Nothing.'

Lance sat up straight suddenly.

'What do you mean, nothing? Don't you care?'

'Of course I care. But I'm prepared to accept things as they are because they can't be changed.'

'Can't we change them?'

'I don't know how. You're too impatient, you know.'

'I can't help wanting to be with you. Even like this. Without sex.'

'I wouldn't want you to split up with your wife.'

'Why not?'

'Don't be silly, darling. You don't want that either. Those things always leave a nasty taste. Friends take sides, your social life is disrupted, you could be ostracised and that would affect your work. Added to which I would have to be introduced into your social orbit and I doubt if I would fit.'

'Why not?'

'Oh, darling! You know why. Besides, I have a career. Remember?'

'Acting.'

'Yes.'

'Wouldn't you give it up?'

'For a special reason, perhaps.'

'What special reason?'

'If I got married, for instance. Which isn't likely to happen.'

'Would you marry me?'

'I would if we could but we can't.'

'At the moment, perhaps.'

'Sweetheart, let's leave it alone. Let's just enjoy each other while we can.'

'I wish I had your strength of mind.'

'You'll go home in a minute and sit and have dinner with your wife and she'll chat with you about her charity works and you will listen and encourage her.'

'It would be charitable if she went away again.'

'You'd still want her back again.'

'Oh, blast!'

They both laughed at Lance's frustration.

When Lance arrived home he was met by a somewhat aggrieved wife.

'You're late,' she said, sternly.

'No, I'm not. This is my normal time.'

'Have you forgotten?'

144

'What?'

'We're due at the Harmans' for dinner.'

'Oh, God! I'd forgotten.'

'Hurry up and change. I'll ring and say we've been held up.'

'Do we have to go?'

'Yes.'

'Why?'

'Because they're important people. To me and to you.'

'Bloody MPs,' muttered Lance as he went upstairs.

He changed into his dinner jacket in a temper. The last thing he wanted was a boring evening with the Harmans, he being their local member of parliament. How much longer was he going to carry on like this? Kay's social life and charitable work was something he used to humour. He didn't feel like humouring anything or anybody at the moment.

The dinner party was as tedious for him as he had anticipated though Kay chatted away and argued and applauded as the case deserved. He drank more than he needed out of sheer boredom. He wasn't interested in the economy of the country or Social Services or the crime rate or global warming. He kept wondering what Helen might be doing. He didn't think she'd stay in the flat on her own. After all, he'd met her in a bar. She had mentioned some kind of Arts Club where people in her profession gathered for drinks and food. Perhaps she would go there, wherever it was.

On the way back from the dinner party Kay remarked, 'You weren't very communicative tonight.'

'Wasn't I?'

'Not your usual self.'

'Sorry.'

145

'Oh, it doesn't worry me. I enjoyed myself. I only wonder what the others thought.'

'I couldn't care less what they thought.'

'You will when it comes to town planning and some of your architectural ideas, housing and so on. The Harmans will be useful then.'

'MPs make promises. They don't get anything done.'

'It's wheels within wheels, dear.'

'I know.'

'Best not put a spoke in them.'

'Huh?'

Kay turned to Lance with concern.

'Are you worried about something?'

'No. Why?'

'You don't seem yourself.'

'I wonder who I am.'

'I'm serious.'

'Don't worry. I'm all right.'

Lance did not want to continue the conversation. Of course he wasn't himself. He knew that. He felt it. He tried to hide the fact but obviously was not succeeding. He could not rid himself of the problem of Helen. She wasn't a problem in herself, far from it. He himself was the problem because he didn't know what to do. Did he want her to be with him all the time? Night and day he wondered. In his mind he went through each day trying to imagine how she would fit in and where she would fit in. Where would they live? Would he separate from Kay? He wouldn't want to get involved in a divorce. That would be fatal both socially and in business. Separation seemed the answer. He imaged leaving her the house. She could afford to run it, she had money of her own. Would he have to live in London because of Helen's work? She had made it quite clear that she did not intend to give up the stage. That was a problem. Could he cope with that? Evenings in the theatre when he wanted her at home. They couldn't go out together during that time. He didn't think he could face that. Perhaps, after all, he should let things stay as they are at the moment. He will have to be satisfied with meeting her at five and leaving at seven, getting home in time for dinner with his wife.

When they went to bed that night Lance noticed how his wife undressed. She didn't take her clothes off in the same way that Helen did. Were there several ways of undressing? Did Helen undress for sex, whereas Kay simply undressed to go to bed? He felt no urge when he saw his wife half-naked. He thought that her flesh looked dull compared to Helen's. It didn't seem to exude anything. It was less shiny. The figures were almost the same. He couldn't find fault with his wife's shape. As she pulled her nightdress over her head and got into bed he was still sitting in the armchair staring into space. They had twin beds so that he need not disturb her. Kay called out as she sat up in bed, 'Aren't you coming to bed?'

'In a minute. I'm having a rest.'

'You can rest in bed.'

'I've got to undress first. That takes up a lot of energy.'

'I can't make you out these days.'

'You shouldn't try.'

'You seem different since I went away.'

'Do I?'

'You're not ill, are you?'

'Not that I know of. Everything is in the right place and in working order.'

147

Lance stood up and began to undress.

'It's the change of life, I expect,' he said.

'Change of something,' muttered Kay as she snuggled down into the bedclothes. 'Goodnight.'

'Goodnight,' echoed Lance, relieved to be left alone.

Kay did not appear to want any attention, not that she ever invited intimacy. She was prepared to put up with Lance's attempts at making love but that aspect of life had been slipping away for some time. He always felt that she regarded it as something to expect, as advised by her mother, rather than something to enjoy. How long had he been married? He tried to remember the days when they weren't married. How did he behave with her? Did he treat her as he treated Helen? He didn't think so. There was physical contact, of course, but more circumspect. Besides, they both knew a lot of mutual friends, which somehow intimidated intentions. Certain things were just 'not done'. What attracted her to him? She was very attractive, of course. And elegant. She was always very elegant no matter where she was or what she was doing. She was always well-turned-out, as you would expect with her social background. Her father was Sir Philip Sidney, an eminent barrister who became an equally eminent judge. Lance wondered if he wasn't impressed by her social background which appealed to the innate snob in every man. They had met at a charity ball in London. They danced a lot but they had never laughed very much. Kay was not an easy laugher. She was so taken up with her charity work, which was at times distressing.

Lance got into bed and stretched out on his back. He stared at the ceiling. What to do? What to do?

When he called at Helen's flat the next day, he had hardly reached the door when it opened suddenly and an excited Helen cried, 'Come in! Come in!'

'I'm coming in,' said Lance.

'Sit down. Sit down.'

'I am sitting down.'

Lance had taken up his position on the sofa. Helen stood triumphantly in front of him.

'I've got a job,' she exclaimed.

'What sort of job?' asked Lance, stupidly.

'Acting, of course.'

'Oh,' said Lance, without enthusiasm.

Helen sat next to him, took his hand in both of hers and pumped it up and down as she emphasised her story.

'I went to an audition this morning and got the part.'

'Good. Well done.'

'The play opens in London after a provincial tour.'

'What does that mean?'

'It means I'll be working for as long as the play lasts.'

'What does it mean for us?'

Helen let go of Lance's hand. She knew that he would not like what she had to say.

'Well, rehearsals start in a couple of weeks which means I may not be here every day at five o'clock.'

'Why not?'

'Depends on the director. Sometimes they like to start at about eleven in the morning and go on till late at night.'

'Oh, no! That means I won't see you.'

'For some of the time.'

'Shit!'

He stood up and paced about the room.

'As soon as the play comes to London we can go back to our five to seven. Because I won't need to be in the theatre until eight o'clock.'

Lance came to a halt in front of Helen.

'Don't do it,' he said.

'What!'

'Don't do it.'

'I must.'

'Why?'

'Because I'm an actress. It's in my blood.'

'Rubbish.'

In his frustration and fear of being without her, Lance reached out and slapped the side of Helen's face with his hand.

'Blast you!' he cried.

Helen's hand went to her face and she looked aghast.

'You hit me.'

'Sorry. Sorry.'

Lance knelt down and hugged her.

'You hit me,' Helen repeated, as if mesmerised.

'I didn't mean to. I don't want you to go. I want you to stay with me. Don't go away, darling. Please.'

Helen guided Lance back to the sofa.

'Now, let's sit quietly and work this out,' she suggested.

'Yes. All right,' agreed Lance, meekly.

'You know, darling, for a grown man, a captain of industry, an important executive, a great achiever, you are like a child.'

'I can't help wanting you.'

'Don't you think I want you, too?'

'Then...'

'There's no "then" about it. Life is life, work is work. What would you say if I made a fuss because

150

you can't come here nine to eleven in the morning? You couldn't do it and I'd have to face it. You managed without me before.'

'I didn't know you. But now I do.'

'Are you prepared to give up your wife?'

'What!'

'Are you?'

'Well, no. I can't at the moment.'

'Then until you do I will continue with my stage career.'

'Is that a threat?'

'Of course not. I'm simply trying to make you see reason. If you can't see me here because I'm rehearsing I suggest, for the sake of your wife, you should kill time in between five and seven for the sake of appearances.'

'You think of everything, don't you?'

'I'm sure your wife would wonder what happened if you got home too early.'

'I hadn't thought of that.'

'You see.'

'You're wonderful. What would I do without you?'

'You're about to find out, dear.'

'No. Don't.'

'Now, don't hit me again.'

'No. Never. Never. I'm so sorry. I was so upset when you told me. I would have kicked my favourite dog.'

'That's not very noble of you.'

'I'm a selfish bastard.'

'I think you are. The trouble is all this is new to you.'

'It is.'

'Rehearsals don't start for a fortnight so we have plenty of time together.

'With a cloud over us.'

'Clouds can be blown away.'

'How?'

'Like this.'

She put her arms round him and kissed him. Their passion overcame them and they slipped from the sofa to the floor again. During their lovemaking Helen murmured the word 'child' but with affection. After that they were able to converse more calmly.

'When rehearsals start,' Lance began, 'will you come back here?'

'Of course. But I won't know exactly when.'

'I could wait for you if I had a key.'

'I'll give you a key. Rehearsal times are usually erratic.'

'I'll put some champagne in the fridge.'

'You don't want to go home pissed.'

'I won't.'

'We can leave messages for each other.'

'That's an idea.'

Later on Lance admitted, 'This chance means a lot to you, doesn't it?'

'Oh, yes. I've been out for some time and I don't want to be forgotten.'

'Then acting isn't so much having something in your blood, as you call it, it's something you must do to be seen. It's wanting to be seen.'

'That doesn't sound very kind.'

'In other words, it's a form of showing off.'

'Darling, you're wearing a suit with a white shirt and a rather spectacular tie. Isn't that showing off? Every time you look in the mirror you're showing off. We all do it.'

'All right. *Touché.*'

'Very *touché* I call it.'

'You know you don't have to worry about money.'

'I'm not going to be a kept woman, dear. Besides, as I age you won't want to see me.'

'That's not true. The same applies to me, anyway.'

'It's different for a man.'

They chatted on aimlessly but to Lance it was like behaving nervously before some disaster. He could not rid himself of the forthcoming void when Helen would no longer be at the flat. He couldn't stop brooding about it no matter how Helen tried to occupy his attention elsewhere. He knew better now than to voice his fears. He was stretched out on the sofa beside her, his legs sticking out over the carpet. They were both very quiet, staring ahead. Helen turned her head casually to look at Lance and could see that he had tears in his eyes. She reached out to him.

'Darling!'

'I don't want you to go,' moaned Lance, tears falling down his cheek. 'I can't help it. I rely on you. You're what I look forward to. I can't do without you. I'm sorry.'

Helen hugged him to her, his face in her breast.

'I won't be far away.'

'It's not the same.'

'I don't know what to say, what to do.'

Lance broke away from her embrace.

'Neither do I.'

He blew his nose loudly. The situation between them was too worrying to be relieved by mere sexual treatment. They could only sit in silence, Lance nursing his grief and Helen wondering how she could help him. At length he looked at his watch.

'Time to go,' he said.

'Oh dear.'

He stood up, holding his hand out to help Helen to her feet. Hand in hand they made their way to the front door. Lance kissed Helen gently on her cheek.

'See you tomorrow.'

'Cheer up.'

Lance made no reply, he simply turned and waved. From her window Helen watched him get into his car. He stood and waved. She waved back. Then he was gone. He'll feel better once he gets home into his own routine, thought Helen. She had no feeling of conquest or triumph or any feeling that a man was so much in love with her. It was too worrying for that. She marvelled at the extreme sensibility of the man. It was almost frightening, even to the point of hitting her. It didn't hurt but it showed how deeply he felt.

Helen was quite wrong about Lance settling into his routine. Driving home he still had that catch in his throat that could turn to tears and when at last he reached his own driveway he thought, 'Oh, God. Back to this.' Fortunately, he was not expected to be demonstrative in any way at home so he greeted his wife as casually as usual. She was just as casual. Anything else was just not done and Lance wouldn't want it any other way. Everything was routine, habit. Kay was not a talkative person except when she was expounding her charity themes. If there was nothing to say then she said nothing. Not like some people that Lance knew who thought that they had to keep chattering in order to be interesting. Thank God, also, for television even if one only sat and complained about the programmes.

* * *

154

Lance and Helen called it their Last Day. At least, that is what Lance called it in his gloomy, masochistic manner. Helen laughed at him for to her the last day, as he called it, was the First Day for her, a step nearer recognition as an actress as it heralded the beginning of rehearsals. Lance allowed himself to be lulled into a happier frame of mind by Helen's enthusiasm and they clung together in their embrace as if they could never be physically separated. They just stayed together breathing and kissing, holding each other tightly, firmly, as if defying anyone to part them. After this evening Lance would visit the flat hopefully and if Helen didn't turn up he would leave a note. These notes were to become quite a collection for Helen also left a note for Lance. The notes were always plaintive, often erotic. But at present they were more concerned about making use of the time that they had before Lance drove home. When the time came to part they both cried, tears playing havoc with Helen's make-up and Lance's usually attractive features creased in an ugly grimace.

After the traumatic parting and the fear of being late for dinner Lance arrived home to find that Kay was out. The housekeeper informed him that madam had put dinner back an hour because she was held up at her committee meeting. Such irony! thought Lance. He could have stayed longer with Helen. He almost rang and told her but they had made a pact about phoning. They would avoid it in case of eavesdroppers.

Lance was told about the reason for the change of dinner time during the meal. It would appear that the committee of whatever charity concern that Kay had been attending were anxious to replace their chairman and, after a good deal of argument and even altercation, it was suggested that Kay should be appointed to the chair. But Kay rejected the offer on the grounds that it would take up too much of her time and take her away from her duties to her husband. Lance could have screamed. Nothing would have pleased him more than to find his wife in more outside pursuits. He told her that she should have taken the position for the prestige if nothing else. But Kay was adamant. She contended that she was not the chairwoman type.

At the flat next day Lance tried to leave a note explaining his frustration and the irony of the situation over the dinner time but all he could say was he could have stayed longer after all. Her note that she had left him simply said that she did not know what time rehearsals would finish. He wanted to phone her but apart from their original pact he did not know the telephone number of the rehearsal room. The only contact that he could make would be on a mobile later in the night in the hope that she would be home. But in order to do that he would have to go into the garden or take refuge in the bathroom. As each escapade would be foreign to his habit, he abandoned the idea to avoid suspicion. Although he admitted to himself that he was leading a double life he was keen to avoid obvious deception.

Helen's notes to Lance were long screeds about the problems at rehearsals. She told him that the director of the play was so fussy that he kept them at it until late at night. None of it interested Lance except when she explained that she could not see any relief until the play actually opened in the West End. That meant that they would have to be content with notes passed to and fro, a notion that did not appeal to Lance. He had imagined that she would be free at least one or two days. He adopted the habit of taking a bottle of champagne to the flat, helping himself and leaving a note which read, 'I've left you some.' She, in turn, left a note thanking him and advising him to be careful driving home after so much champagne, which she had noted from the amount left in the bottle.

Rehearsals were in their second week when Lance left a note at the flat saying, 'How much bloody longer?' The answer did not please him. Helen wrote at length to say that rehearsals would be over by the end of the week but they would be followed by a provincial try-out at Birmingham for another week. There was a chance to meet, however, during the weekend before Birmingham. Could Lance manage it? No. He couldn't. He and Helen had never met at weekends and his could not think of an excuse to leave home without causing suspicion. It was now Helen's turn to be frustrated. She knew that they had never met at weekends and that Lance could not plead pressure of business in order to be in his office because such a thing had never happened before. They would not be able to exchange notes during the provincial tour unless Helen addressed a letter to herself advising Lance to open it. It was the nearest they could get to each other but the idea was abandoned because it was considered that by the time the letter arrived Helen would probably be back home.

Kay found Lance morose and silent and wondered why.

'Are you all right?' she asked.

'What?'

'Are you all right?'

'Yes. Why?'

'You're very quiet.'

'I feel quiet.'

'I wondered if you were feeling ill or something.'

'No.'

They were at dinner, just the two them and, in fact, Lance was brooding over the loss of Helen and the futility of trying to make sense of his life all the while the theatre was hanging over them. He wanted to say to Kay, 'For Christ's sake leave me alone.' He couldn't tell her that he was missing Helen. The provincial tour had created complete isolation. It wasn't even worth going to the flat. There could be no contact. Again he asked himself what did she mean to him. Why did he feel like this? Why did he want her to be around so much? He just wanted to be with her, not even talking. He wasn't interested in the theatre. He found plays boring and Kay knew it so it would be a fatal admission if he said he wanted to see a play just because Helen was in it. He had known other women and had brief affairs with them. But they never meant the same to him as Helen did. Why? He did not want to marry her any more than she wanted to marry him. They understood that. What, then, was the answer? Go on as they are? Not if the stage keeps getting in the way. He knew, though, that he could not give her up. Did it mean that the only happiness in his life would be between the hours of five and seven in the evening? How did Helen herself feel about that, he wondered. Wasn't it making a bit of a prostitute of her? Except that he was her only customer and he never paid her. He could never be certain how she felt. She appeared to be so self-reliant, so self-assured. How would she feel if he left her, which he would never do. She had never told him. What difference would it make to her? Very little, he imagined. After all, he met her sitting on a stool in the American Bar of a smart hotel. Since then she had been a great help and comfort to him. She almost mothered him.

In addition to his mood of depression, Kay noticed that he was arriving home earlier than usual. She was not to know that he did not know what to do with himself while the Birmingham tour was in progress. He couldn't just sit around drinking. He had his club in London, of course, but he seldom used it. It was an all-male club and he did not fancy that type of company at the moment. The last thing he fancied was being hearty.

And then came the day when Helen arrived back at the flat. Lance raced up the stairs, ignoring the lift. He let himself in with his key, fumbling so much in his agitation that it was eventually opened by Helen. Lance fell into her hall breathless. He picked Helen up and hugged her and they fell on the floor as they were, laughing together. They did not attempt to make love. There was too much to talk about. Helen was full of her theatre news but all Lance seemed to be able to say was, 'I missed you. I missed you.' Once they had relaxed and were lounging on their famous sofa, Helen said they could now go back to their five to seven routine because her appearance in the theatre was not necessary until eight o'clock.

'I feel safe again now,' said Lance.

'Let's hope we have a long run,' said Helen.

'You mean the play?'

'Both.'

'I don't want to go through all that again.'

'Not until the next play.'

'Oh, no! Don't say that.'

'My agent is suddenly enthusiastic.'

'Tell him not to be.'

'I don't suppose for one moment I'll be mentioned in the reviews but my director was very complimentary during rehearsals.'

'Is he after you?'

'Him? He's as gay as a peacock.'

'You say that about everyone in the theatre.'

'It's true. They're all gay.'

'And are all the women lessies?'

'You should know about that, dear. You've been with me long enough.'

'In other words, if this play doesn't run very long you may find yourself in another one.'

'Well, that's the profession.'

'Bloody nuisance.'

'I can't refuse a play.'

'You can. You can say it's not good enough.'

'That would brand me as what is known as a difficult artist, which would be death to my career.'

'Does this one feel like a long run? You can tell, can't you?'

'It's got the feel, yes.'

'Fingers crossed.'

'You dread the thought don't you?'

'I certainly do.'

'But here we are together again. It's not as if I wasn't coming back.'

'I can't explain.'

'I can. I'm afraid you're a little spoilt, darling.'

'Eh?'

'If you don't get your own way you stamp your little foot.'

'That's what you think of me, is it?'

'It's part of your charm, darling.'

'Except when I hit you.'

'I don't think you'll do that again.'

'I know I won't.'

Their short evening ended happily, lovingly, as if she had never been away and Lance forgot all of his former misery.

In fact, Kay found him gay and jovial when he arrived home that night. It was a complete change from the brooding image of the previous week. She knew better than to comment on it. She never questioned him about his work but knew that at times he had problems getting his plans accepted by certain government departments. She had suggested a holiday when he was so miserable but he said he couldn't spare the time when in fact he did not want to be anywhere that Helen could not identify with him. It was a long time since he had smelt the sea. He did not even want to go to his favourite city – Venice. Kay had recently been to Australia so she couldn't complain when he didn't want to go away. She was thinking of his health. She didn't want him to have a breakdown through overwork.

One warm sunny evening Lance had the urge to sit in the nearby Green Park instead of staying in the flat. The park was only a matter of a few hundred yards away and he thought that Helen would like

161

some air for a change. He fancied sitting with her in a couple of deckchairs.

'Aren't you afraid of being seen?' asked Helen.

'We've been seen,' said Lance.

'Where?'

'When we first met at the bar. Twice.'

'That was nothing.'

'Anyone who knows me would more likely see me in a bar than a deckchair in the park.'

And that was his mistake. He was seen and did not know it. They were sitting in the area of Green Park which abuts Piccadilly. A pathway crossed the park from the corner of the Ritz Hotel to the other side and it is a good short cut for people who want to reach the Grosvenor Place area and Constitution Hill. There is plenty of space in the park, acres of it and in the fine weather deckchairs abound. Lance and Helen found a cluster of three in a line and promptly sat down in two of them.

'That's better,' said Lance, taking a deep breath. 'Fresh air.'

'My place isn't all that stuffy, is it?'

'Darling, your place is heaven. So is this.'

They sat facing the setting sun and Lance felt that he could have been in his own garden with Helen beside him. It was so enjoyable and peaceful that they visited the park more than once, returning to the flat for a farewell embrace.

Kay was happy that Lance was happy and she left it at that. Until the occasion of one of her committee meetings when a fellow member asked her, in casual conversation, if she enjoyed herself in the park.

'Park?' said Kay. 'What park?'

162

'Green Park. You know. The one that runs beside Piccadilly.'

The lady would have continued with her story if the chairman had not called the members to order and there was no chance of further conversation until after the meeting.

The lady who raised the subject of the park was Madge Parker, a middle-aged do-gooder known to her friends as Nosey Parker because that was the sort of person she was. They regarded her as a gossip and she was not particularly liked. She lived in London in the Kensington area. She appeared on several committees all over the country and was very generous with her donations and time. She was a rich widow.

When this particular meeting was over Kay made a point of finding Madge and asked her, 'What did you mean about the park, Madge?'

'Weren't you sitting in a deckchair with Lance in Green Park the other evening?'

'I've never been in Green Park.'

'There were three chairs in a row. Lance was in the middle, there was a girl I didn't recognise on one side and the other chair was empty. I presumed you'd got up and gone away for something.'

'No. Not me. You're sure it was Lance?'

'Oh, yes. I wasn't far away. I often take that short cut across the park.'

'It was definitely Lance?'

'Oh, yes. He was chatting with the girl.'

'That doesn't mean anything. Just striking up a conversation. Particularly if the chairs were close, as you say. It would have been rude to move a chair away.'

'I quite thought you weren't far away.'

'No. I've never been there.'

'It's nowhere near Lance's office, is it?'

'He doesn't stay in the office. He moves all over London. You should have stopped and talked to him.'

'I didn't like to.'

Kay gave a little laugh.

'That's not like you, Madge.'

'Besides, I was in a hurry.'

'You could have waved.'

'He didn't look my way. He was busy chatting to the girl.

'An evening in the park sounds a nice idea,' concluded Kay. 'I must try it sometime.'

With that she walked away and as Madge watched her go she thought how naïve the lady was for all her committee work. Now she knew that Kay had not been in the park with Lance it was obvious that some kind of liaison was going on between Lance and that girl. As she remembered the two of them together it was certainly not the mere starting up of a conversation, as Kay had suggested. It looked more intimate than that. Poor Kay, she thought.

It wasn't a matter of poor Kay, as Madge thought. Kay may have sounded as though she couldn't care less, however, she was actually quite upset and not a little angry. She had butterflies in her stomach at the thought of Lance picking up a girl, which is what Madge made it sound like. The girl, whoever she was, could not have been someone he knew. That was out of the question, she was sure. But what did it mean? Why should Lance be in the park at all?

When Lance arrived home that evening Kay said nothing about Madge's remark. Madge, she knew, was an awful gossip. Everybody knew that. If Lance was in the park, which seemed unlikely in itself, he must have had a reason for going there. She did not

164

accept that any girl was concerned. She watched Lance as he ate his evening meal and tried to discover if Madge's suggestion could be possible. She just couldn't imagine it. It was so out of character and it wasn't like him. It was almost laughable. Madge must have mistaken him for somebody like him. Why should Lance be sitting in the park unless he wanted to study some nearby building or contemplate some aspect of the park itself. She remembered how he had envisaged the theme park at Norton Towers. That was quite an achievement and is still enjoyed by thousands of visitors.

When Lance again suggested to Helen that they sat in the park she asked, 'Are you getting tired of me?'

'Tired of you? Don't be silly.'

'At one time you were content to lie naked with me here.'

'I still am.'

'But not for so long. Are you going off me?'

'Good Lord, no! It's just that I don't like to keep you in a cage all the time. I'd like to be out and about with you.'

'I still think it's a risk.'

'What kind of risk?'

'It only needs someone to see you and tell your wife.'

'No one saw us last time.'

'There's always a first time.'

'If you don't want to go...'

'Oh, I'll go. I love sitting out in the sun. I'm only worried for you.'

'Don't worry. Let's get some air.'

As they relaxed in their deckchairs in the park

165

they were again seen by Madge who was taking her usual short cut across the park. She stopped and looked at Lance and then walked on, looking back now and then to reassure herself. She was not mistaken, she decided, no matter how Kay protested. Lance was no look-alike. That was Lance himself. And with the same girl. There could be no doubt about it. She could not wait to tell Kay when they next met, if only to justify her previous assertion.

Lance and Helen were blissfully unaware of Madge's reaction. Lance didn't even know her except as a name among Kay's charity workers. Helen was only fearful for Lance's sake. She didn't want him to have trouble with his wife.

Trouble, unfortunately, was in the offing.

'I saw them again,' said Madge as she met Kay at another committee meeting.

'What are you talking about?' asked Kay, testily.

'Lance and that girl. They were in the park in their deckchairs again. I didn't think I was wrong last time.'

'Why are you telling me?'

'I thought you should know.'

'Should?'

'Would like.'

'Well, I wouldn't. I'm sure there's a perfectly reasonable explanation.'

'You're not worried that he might be having an affair?'

'Good Heavens, no!'

'I would be.'

'Because he's sitting in the park in a deckchair next to some girl.'

'They seemed quite intimate.'

'How can you tell?'

'They were holding hands.'

'How shocking.'

Kay laughed as she walked away from her friend. In reality, though, she was far from levity. She was worried and not a little angry. Why should Lance be in the park in the first place? Her idea that he might be contemplating some theme park did not hold water. As for holding hands with a girl, that didn't fit in either. Perhaps there was something in Madge's gossip, though she would never admit it to her. When she thought of the possibility of Lance being unfaithful she had a sinking feeling in her stomach and felt an anger build up in her. Should she tackle Lance with an accusation? How? What could she say? Would he deny it or would he explain what it all meant? It had not affected her in any way. He was just as caring and thoughtful as he ever was. They didn't indulge in a lot of sex these days but that seemed to be a mutual acceptance. She could take it or leave it. There was never any urge about it. She had always presumed that Lance felt the same way. Unless he'd got what could be called a second wind. Then things did happen with men, she believed. In which case, surely, he would come to her. None of this she would ever discuss with anyone, least of all with Madge. She would keep it to herself. But there was anger smouldering inside her. She did not know what to think.

At dinner that night she particularly watched Lance.

'Lance,' she said. 'You've developed a tan from somewhere.'

'Have I? You can't help it this weather.'

'Have you been sitting in the sun?'

'Yes. When I can.'

'Where?'

'In the park mostly.'

'On your own?'

'Well, no. There are a lot of people there.'

'I meant were you with someone.'

'No.'

He knew that he was lying but Kay didn't.

'Why do you go in the park?'

'I find it relaxing.'

'It's nowhere near the office.'

'I drive there.'

'You could drive home and sit in the garden.'

'I like watching people. I wonder about them, what their lives are like.'

'Have you ever seen Madge go by?'

'Who?'

'Madge Parker.'

'I wouldn't know her. I only know her as a name you sometimes mention.'

'She's seen you there.'

'In the park?'

'Yes. She takes a short cut across there.'

'Oh, I know the one. Starts by the Ritz.'

'That's right.'

'She says she's seen you twice.'

'Quite likely.'

'She thought I was with you the first time because evidently there were three chairs together, one occupied by a young woman.'

'You can't always get one right away. You have to sit near someone.'

'She says the same woman was there each time.'

'That's possible.'

'You were holding hands.'

'That's not possible. I'm not the hand-holding type. As you know.'

'I do. Yes.'

Kay was still worried. This was verbal fencing and she felt that Lance was not being completely truthful. He was hiding behind a kind of badinage, making light of something he was obviously trying to hide. She decided to drop the subject at the moment for fear of some kind of rift in their partnership and they both went to bed happily and separately. Kay convinced herself that there was nothing to worry about.

The one person who was not convinced was Madge Parker. She watched for Lance as she took her usual short cut across the park. But he wasn't there. She lingered. She did not think that she could have been mistaken. She even sat in a deckchair and waited. He had been there two days running so surely he would come again.

Lance was in the flat with Helen and as they sat on the sofa together she asked, casually, 'No park today?'

'No. We've been seen.'

'Oh, my God!'

Helen sat upright suddenly.

'I was afraid of that. Who saw us?'

'Some busybody friend of Kay.'

'Did you get into trouble?'

'No. I managed to bluff my way through it. I admitted I was in the park but on my own. I said I often go there.'

'Did it work?'

'I think so. No more was said.'

'We'd better stay in, then.'

'No. What I'm going to do is sit in the park on

my own so that when this woman goes by she'll see that there's no one with me.'

'Do you know her?'

'No. Never seen her. I only know her as a name on one of Kay's committees.'

'Then how will you know if she sees you?'

'I'll have to trust to luck.'

'You'll come back here?'

'Oh, yes. I won't be long.'

He got up from the sofa, leaned over, gave Helen a peck on the cheek and left the flat.

He made for the park where he sat in a deckchair and hoped that this Madge what's-her-name would go by. Actually, she was waiting not far away. She watched him as he sat down on his own. She wondered if the girl would join him. She did not believe that he would just sit there on his own. But no girl did join him. Madge could not understand it. When, at length, Lance got up to leave she decided to follow him. She saw him leave the park and make for one of the roads that ran parallel to it behind Piccadilly. It was called Gloucester Gardens. She saw Lance enter a block of flats. Knowing that he did not know her, she followed him into the vestibule, saw him press a button for the lift that took him to the third floor. Once the lift had ascended she went to the entrance of the building where the names of the tenants were displayed. She noted that number three belonged to Helen Forrest. Who was Helen Forrest, she wondered. She had never heard Kay mention her. How could she find out who the girl was? She left the building and wandered aimlessly along the road until she came to a newsagent shop. She stopped. She went in.

A man behind the counter said, 'Yes?'

'Excuse me, I wonder if you can help me. I'm looking for a Helen Forrest. I was told she lived in this road.'

'Helen Forrest, the actress?' said the man. 'Third floor of that block of flats over there.'

He pointed to the building that Madge had just left.

'Thank you,' said Madge. 'Very kind of you.'

'No trouble.'

Trust a newsagent to know where people live and their trade, thought Madge. So that's who the girl was. She walked back to the block of flats and stood on the other side of the road waiting for Lance to come out.

Lance was telling Helen that they had to find somewhere else to breathe the fresh air.

'You're determined to get out, aren't you?' she said.

'I'm thinking of you cooped up here all day.'

'I'm used to it.'

'I know,' said Lance, suddenly. 'We'll take the car and watch the ducks in St James' Park. Come on.'

'Wait a minute. I'll get some bread for them.'

'Good idea.'

Madge saw them leave together and make for the car which was parked nearby. She recognised the girl as the one in the deckchair. She could not wait to tell Kay of her discovery.

The opportunity occurred at the next committee meeting. When the meeting broke up Madge found Kay and took her arm to lead her aside.

'Kay, I must talk to you.'

'What now?' asked Kay, testily.

'I've seen Lance in the park again.'

'Oh?'

'He was on his own.'

'Is that surprising?'

'Well, it is actually.'

'Why?'

'I think you must have spoken to him.'

'I did mention it.'

Kay was determined to be off-hand with Madge.

'I got the impression that he was showing that he was alone. I'll tell you why; because when he got up to leave I followed him.'

'Oh, Madge. Why?'

'I was curious.'

'He probably got in the car and drove away.'

'But he didn't. He walked round the corner to a block of flats in Gloucester Gardens.'

'You followed him all that way?'

'It's only round the corner. I saw him go up to the third floor and on the name board outside, number three belongs to Helen Forrest.'

'You found all that out?'

'Yes. And more.'

Kay could feel the colour changing in her cheeks and she hoped that it didn't show. She must behave as if she didn't care when in fact she felt sick at heart.

'Helen Forrest,' said Madge, 'is an actress.'

'How do you know?'

'The newsagent along the road told me.'

'You went and asked who she was?'

'I simply asked where Helen Forrest lived.'

'But you knew. You saw the name on the building, you said.'

'I was going to ask him about her but there was no need. He told me.'

'Madge, you're a proper Miss Marple.'

'I was thinking of you, dear. I don't like you being two-timed.'

'Neither do I.'

'When Lance came out of the building he was with the girl I'd seen him with before.'

'Where did they go?'

'They got in the car and drove away. I don't know where they went.'

'You didn't run after them?'

'It's not funny, Kay.'

'I know it's not. You don't have to tell me.'

'What are you going to do about it?'

'I'll talk to Lance, of course. He may have an explanation.'

'Yes. And I can imagine what it is,' scoffed Madge as she walked away and found other members of the committee who sat drinking coffee.

Kay would usually join them and take part in any discussion but on this occasion she left the building at once. She may not have shown it with Madge but she was seething with anger. How dare Lance behave in such a disreputable way, humiliating her in the process? He was obviously having an affair with this Helen Forrest woman. What was he doing with an actress, of all people? How did he meet her? He had lied when she questioned him before. But now she had some real evidence and she meant to confront him with it in no uncertain way.

Lance arrived home blissfully unaware of the reception he was about to receive. He found Kay in the drawing room idly turning the pages of a magazine.

'Hello, dear,' he said, in greeting.

'Hello,' said Kay, icily. 'How was Helen Forrest?'

'I beg your pardon?'

'You're a liar, Lance.'

'Oh?'

'Admit it. You've been with her, haven't you?'

'I...'

'Madge has told me all about it. She saw you in the park again but on your own.'

'That's right.'

'But not for long. You crept round to Gloucester Gardens to a block of flats on the third floor occupied by an actress named Helen Forrest. She was the one you were in the park with on the two previous occasions.'

'You're well-informed.'

'How do you suppose I feel being told that my husband is a liar and adulterer? Can you imagine my humiliation? An affair taking place right under my nose. I daren't face the committee again. Thanks to you, you utter shit.'

'That's going a bit far.'

'Admit it. Go on. Admit it.'

'I admit I've been seeing Helen Forrest, but...'

'Sleeping with her. Fucking her.'

'You're not behaving like the cool, collected committee member, dear.'

'And never will be again, having been made a fool of.'

'Darling, it happens to a lot of people.'

'What does?'

'Men. Going off.'

'Oh, I'm supposed to take it in my stride, am I?'

'I don't mean that.'

'Well, I won't and I intend to sue for a divorce.'

'No. Don't do that.'

'Why not? Afraid it might upset your social position, affect your business? I bloody well hope it does and I hope the whole squalid mess comes out in court.'

174

'Please, Kay. Don't do that. Let's talk it over.'

'Too late. I've made up my mind.'

'You're going too far over a mere peccadillo.'

'Nothing is mere about adultery.'

'Oh, God. Kay, I beg you...'

'You can beg as much as you like. I'll never get over the humiliation you've caused me.'

'What humiliation? You're the only one who knows.'

'Only one? The whole committee knows after Madge has finished with them and it'll go on from there.'

'On the strength of one woman's gossip?'

'Which happens to be the truth, not gossip.'

'You'll ruin me if you divorce me.'

'Serves you right.'

'Now you're being vicious.'

'Lance, if I had a gun I'd shoot you.'

'Christ!'

Kay heaved herself angrily out of the chair and made to go out of the room.

'Where are you going?'

'Upstairs. To pack.'

'Kay!'

Lance followed her out of the room and up the stairs to the landing where he caught up with her, took her arm and stopped her.

'Kay! Please!'

'Get out of my way.'

Kay pushed Lance away as he stood at the top of the stairs barring her way. He staggered back a pace from the impact and then came forward and took her by the shoulders.

'Listen to me, Kay.'

'No!'

They struggled for a position at the top of the stairs until suddenly Kay let out a cry and fell headlong to the bottom, landing in a grotesque position and quite still. Lance had not pushed her, she simply lost her balance because they were locked together.

Lance raced down the stairs, leant over Kay's body and tried to pick her up but she was dead. He called out to the kitchen, 'Maria! Joseph! Help!'

Both the housekeeper and the houseman came running into the hall.

'Madam's fallen down the stairs,' cried Lance. 'Get the doctor, Joseph. Quick!'

Joseph went to the telephone while Lance and Maria tried to revive his wife.

'Poor madam,' moaned Maria.

When the doctor arrived he pronounced Kay dead. 'How did it happen?' he asked.

'I don't know,' admitted Lance. 'I was in the drawing room. She'd gone upstairs for something, I don't know what. I suppose she was on her way down to dinner. I heard a thud, I went out into the hall and there she was. She must have tripped on the stairs.'

Lance knew that he was lying but his explanation was accepted and the whole thing was regarded as an unfortunate accident. The newspapers carried stories of a famous architect's wife falling to her death. At the office everyone was kind and sympathetic. Lance thanked his lucky stars.

Helen read the story in the newspaper and wondered how it had happened and what would happen now. Lance was a free person again. Is that what he wanted? Would it mean that he would want to become more involved with her? She did not want him to cling to her too much. Would he want to marry her? She did not want that.

She anticipated that Lance would stay away from her until the reaction to his wife's death had calmed down. It would be rather blatant if he came round straight away. He'll probably wait until after the funeral.

Which is what he did. Lance was tempted to phone Helen after the accident but resisted in order to avoid any possible insinuation. She must realise that he had to be careful. People talk. He had to admit to himself that he killed his wife. Although he did it accidentally, he was nevertheless responsible for her death. He didn't actually push her down the stairs but he was the cause of their struggling on the landing. He was trying to stop her coming up and in so doing caused her to fall. Could he have saved her? If he'd grabbed her arm as she was falling could he have saved her? He lied about being in the drawing room at the time when in fact he hurried down the stairs to be in front of her. If he hadn't done that the police would have been called and he would have become involved in some awkward questioning.

It was a week after the funeral that Helen heard the bell ring in her flat. She opened the door to admit Lance. Without a word he went in, put his arms round her and hugged her.

'Darling!' cried Helen, quietly.

'Don't say anything,' said Lance.

They sat together on the sofa holding hands.

'I want everything to be as it was before,' said Lance. 'I will still live at home and come here as usual between five and seven. Is that all right with you?'

'Of course.'

'I couldn't ring you.'

'I know.'

'I don't feel like it yet.'

She knew what he meant.

'Neither do I,' she admitted.

'Let's just sit.'

After a silence Helen asked, 'Why didn't you use your key?'

'I forgot.'

They both laughed.

It was on the second visit that Lance said, 'It's such a lovely day why don't we go and sit in the park?'

'But...'

'It's all right. There's nothing to worry about now.'

As they sat in their respective deckchairs no one was to know what thoughts were going through their heads. Lance felt that he was now able to contend with Helen's absence when she was away. Helen felt relieved that their togetherness was not impaired. They were happy in their own way.